The Throttlepenny Murder

Roger J. Green

OXFORD
UNIVERSITY PRESS

OXFORD

UNIVERSITY PRESS

Great Clarendon Street, Oxford OX2 6DP

Oxford University Press is a department of the University of Oxford.
It furthers the University's objective of excellence in research, scholarship,
and education by publishing worldwide in

Oxford New York

Athens Auckland Bangkok Bogotá Buenos Aires Calcutta
Cape Town Chennai Dar es Salaam Delhi Florence Hong Kong Istanbul
Karachi Kuala Lumpur Madrid Melbourne Mexico City Mumbai
Nairobi Paris São Paulo Singapore Taipei Tokyo Toronto Warsaw

and associated companies in Berlin Ibadan

Oxford is a registered trade mark of Oxford University Press
in the UK and in certain other countries

Copyright © Roger J. Green 1989

The moral rights of the author have been asserted

First published 1989
Reprinted 1990
First published in this edition 1999

British Library Cataloguing in Publication Data available

ISBN 0 19 275052 6

Typeset by AFS Image Setters Ltd, Glasgow
Printed in Great Britain by Cox & Wyman Ltd, Reading, Berkshire

'LOOKING BACK, I should have been much more severe with Jessie Smith. Her name only appeared twice in my school Punishment Book. It should have appeared more often. Miss White, my assistant teacher, should have caned her so hard that she would have realized the difference between right and wrong, and then the murder would never have happened.'

Mr M. Middlemas J.P.
Jessie Smith's ex-headmaster

10th of January 1885 price 1d

THE LAMBTON ECHO

THE MURDER that took place in Lambton last week of the worthy and upright Mr. Ezekiel Dobson was one of the most horrible and vile murders that this County of Derbyshire has ever seen. It was one that will stain the history of the fair town of Lambton for ever.

That a mere child, a young maid of thirteen years old, is now in prison and awaiting trial is another sad blemish upon the people who inhabit this most fair and honest town.

The old man was brutally battered to death. No other suspect has been arrested. The readers of this journal must ask themselves what is happening to this fair country of ours when such a vile murder can take place. Are our children being educated too much? The young maid now in prison had free schooling from the age of five to twelve. Now she may hang for murder. Readers must ask themselves these and many more questions about this most terrible of all murders.

For my mother, Margaret Green,
who used to tell me stories about
giggling in school and becoming
the enemy of schoolteachers.

CHAPTER
[1]

JESSIE SMITH had never really meant to harm the old man.
Certainly she had never really meant to kill him. Not really.
Yes, it was true she hated him, but no more than many
children hate grown-ups who behave unpleasantly towards
them. The hatred had seemed harmless. An everyday
feeling that somehow became mixed up with forces that got
out of control.

She had dreamed seemingly harmless day-dreams about
punishing the old man. Sometimes, when he had been
really mean to her, she had imagined finishing him off, but
mostly the day-dreams were harmless ones like pouring a
bucket of cold cow muck over his head until only his glasses
gleamed out of the muck like twin pale pebbles. But kill
him? Murder him? It could not be said that she had
deliberately set out to murder him, though that was said
against her by the Judge.

Jessie Smith was just thirteen years old. She worked in
the shop of Ezekiel Dobson, a high-class grocer in the
market town of Lambton: a fine shop where the rich folk
sent their servants to buy their coffee beans, cheese, butter,
and sugar biscuits; where the richer farmers' wives bought
supplies for the long Derbyshire winters. Jessie had left
school when she was twelve, and she had now worked for
the old man for three months. Three months! It seemed like
a lifetime to Jessie, much longer than her life at school
which had lasted seven years. School had been bad enough,
but working for the old man was much worse. The old man
was mean to her in a thousand ways, and paid her a poor
wage of sixpence a day. Yet she put up with it. The shop
was just a few streets away from her mam and dad and her

1

baby brothers. And it was a shop job, better than working in the open fields as a farm girl, or in the dusty cotton mill of Arkwrights a mile up the road.

It was the old man's meanness of mind and spirit that wore Jessie down so. Although his grocer's shop was a dim cave of treasures—ruby red hams, faded pillars of old gold cheeses, fat-bellied barrels of emerald green pippins, diamond-glassed cases of glittering sugar biscuits—Ezekiel Dobson was the most miserly man in Lambton. Even the townsfolk called him 'Throttlepenny' behind his back. To his face, like Jessie, they called him Mister Dobson. But when he had been murdered, the townspeople forgot he was called Ezekiel Dobson and talked for years to come about the Throttlepenny Murder and Jessie Smith.

Before his murder, Jessie had had to put up with him from 8 o'clock in the morning until 8 o'clock at night. She had had only one thing to help her through the day, and that was her dreams. For Jessie was a great day-dreamer. Perhaps it was the power of these dreams that brought about the murder . . . for dreams, like wishes, are powerful forces. Jessie herself came to realize that herself when it was too late.

She had three dreams for her armour against the old man. The first one consisted of ways to punish him, such as locking him in the disused bread oven across the shop yard and feeding him with poisoned bread through the rusty grill. Dangerous thoughts. Her second day-dream was about her boyfriend, big John Mellor, who was the same age as she was. He had been in her class at school and he now worked at Blackdon Castle as a stable boy. She sometimes saw him on his nights off, twice a month. As she cut the cold and slimy cheeses with the cheese wire, measured out the raisins, brown and plump with damp like brown maggots, she day-dreamed of her sweetheart a lot. Now it was January, she dreamed she was sledging down an endless white and silver lane, her arms tight round John, and as she hugged him the stars shimmered and the moon danced. As they sledged, they passed old Ezekiel Dobson trudging through a swirling blizzard, crying, 'Dunna leave me to die, Jessie. I need ye now. Come back, my dear. I'll

2

be kind to thee from now on.' But she left him to die . . . It was the third dream that excited her most and so was the most powerful and dangerous. It was a ghost story dream. Jessie believed in ghosts and devils. Hadn't she and John seen one in the woods on that never-to-be-forgotten day just over a year ago? She shivered as she weighed the hissing white sugar from the barrel into blue bags, imagining ghosts, boggarts, monsters, devils, witches, all tormenting the old man. She imagined them eating him whole, as she chopped the old butter barrels up, or grinding his bones, as she turned the wheel of the huge coffee-bean grinder. As the devils tormented him, so the old man called for help in the dream. Sometimes Jessie went to his help. Sometimes she did not. And it is strange how so very often dreams and wishes come true.

Jessie took the axe to the shop with her on Monday the 5th of January 1885. It was Market Day and she was rushed off her feet the moment the squeaking hinges of the door swung it open at 8 o'clock in the morning. Jessie shivered as she opened the door.

Throttlepenny had decided to go and see a Cheese Factor and a Chandler, six miles away, in a lonely village. He wanted to complain about the quality of the Christmas cheese and candles. He made a hobby of complaining and grumbling. He also enjoyed leaving Jessie to struggle with a hundred or more Market Day customers. He knew she would not get into any mischief. It was safer to leave her in a crowded shop than an empty one. And he had no fears that she would not serve properly. Jessie was good at her work. He took advantage of that.

So the old man had departed with a clatter of hooves on the frosty road, in a hired pony and trap from the Anchor Inn. Jessie was left in the shop with the customers and a mind full of dreams. Jessie smiled, nodded and sometimes curtsied, as the old man had taught her, pinching her bottom to assist the learning. The gold that Throttlepenny so loved trickled into the cash drawer. As the gold coins grew, so did Jessie's dreams. She imagined Throttlepenny's horse and trap suddenly plunging over the edge of a bridge, and the old man being swept away, his head bobbing in the slate grey water, crying, 'I'm sorry I were cruel to ye, Jessie.' Then from the bank John Mellor would dive in and rescue him, and they'd all go to Throttlepenny's house for cocoa and be given a gold sov each, and Jessie and John would walk back hand in hand and be happy ever after. The dreams sometimes did end without violence. For Jessie, in her heart of hearts, could not understand how other people could not love like she did.

The day sped on. She weighed out Garibaldi biscuits with their little black currants, like dried flies. She weighed out coffee into salmon pink bags that said, E. DOBSON. PURVEYOR OF FINE COFFEES TO THEIR GRACES THE DUKES OF BLACKDON AND PEMBERLY. She weighed out Bath biscuits, warm and white as pebbles in a summer river, and dreamed a new exciting dream of the ghostly kind. Throttlepenny was in the churchyard putting flowers on his dead wife's grave. Out popped a shining and luminous devil, his skeleton glowing through his devilish skin. He tucked Throttlepenny under his arm. Jessie shivered happily as she put a brass half-pound weight on the scales. 'I know you're taking me to Hell because I've been right nasty to Jessie,' called Throttlepenny to the devil. Then he called to Jessie and John, holding hands close by. 'Tell God, Jessie, I'm right sorry. Let me stay and I'll buy thee and John a little cottage with honeysuckle round the door, a little love nest for thee both.' This pleased Jessie and she dreamed it many times. Perhaps that gave it power.

Dusk fell. The lamplighter had lit the gas lamp outside in the street. The old man had not returned. It became suddenly quiet in the shop. It was then that her dreams of devils and ghosts were given a strange air of reality when her Aunty Lily Gosling waddled into the shop. Her great aunt had waited until the shop was quiet.

'Hello, Jessie my love. I've come to buy in. It's getting colder. We're in for a cold spell. An' summat bad's going to happen. There's signs all round.'

Jessie paused in her weighing of nose-tickling tea. This sounded good. Her aunt was a superstitious woman, a big believer in spirits, fortune telling, ghosts and the super-natural. Jessie beamed at her aunt. She felt like a good story. She might even use it for a dream. Or frighten Throttlepenny with it when he returned. The old lady dusted the shop chair with a corner of her shawl, sniffed and sat down. With a quick look over her shoulder to see nobody was coming, the old lady hoisted her dress up and warmed her giant white legs by the fire with a sigh of pleasure. Jessie could see a good tale was coming.

'Weigh us two pounds of raisins, Jessie. Keep 'em under a shilling, love. Well, they've been seen. Them stone walkers.' Jessie knew better than to interrupt. She gripped the brass pound weight that was so cold it stung her like a springtime nettle. 'It's them stone devils, Jessie, carved on church tower. Tha knows—just below t'spire. Gargoyles or gumboils, folk wi' schooling calls 'em. They're stone devils to me, Jess. Anyhow, them stone devils is restless, Jess. I'll tell thee what I've heard.' She smiled with pleasure at Jessie's wide-eyed wonder. Jessie was one of her best audiences.

'And a pun of sugar, Jessie. Aye. Them devils is about in the town.' Jessie shivered. She thought of her dream about the devil taking Throttlepenny. Then she had a quick dream of a devil hitting Throttlepenny with the axe she had brought to work. But her great aunt was talking. 'It's the cold that stirs up magic, Jess. And all winter magic is done on old St. Thomas's Day. That were last Friday. It were the day after Old Lizzy telled me t'devils were walking the town. Me, I'm not surprised, all that's been going off in this parish the last year or two. Old Lizzy said she'd heard them laughing. It fair puts a chill in your heart, Jess, to think of them devils laughing in t'churchyard when nobody's there but the spirits of the dead. Aye. They'm laughing. Cold's cracking their faces into laughter, Jess.'

Jessie's eyes shone. She imagined the terrified Throttle-penny being attacked by a devil with an axe, and being rescued by Jessie. The old lady, seeing her face, embroidered the tale.

'They say one of the devil's come off altogether, Jess. He's walking the town flapping his cloak like a nesting

5

jackdaw an' laughing like a nickopecker in spring. Something bad's going to happen.'

There was silence in the shop. What a story. Jessie could see it all. The stone figure looming in the gaslight outside the door, holding out his stone fingers for the axe that lay in Jessie's bag.

Aunty Lily fingered a wart on her face that grew a single tough black hair. Her seamed old face arranged itself in a pleased smile. 'Old Throttlepenny ought to be careful, love. Him with all that gold. He's worth taking!' She laughed and Jessie laughed. Jessie handed over the blue bag of sugar, an amber one of sultanas, and a red one of raisins. The old lady handed over a silver florin. Jessie leaned over the counter and kissed the old lady's face, hot and dry with old age, under the shawl. She kissed her again. What a story to dream about. This was the stuff of dreams. The old lady smiled and shuffled out. She was to remember Jessie's last kiss to the end of her days.

She turned at the door. 'I knew trouble were brewing when I hung up me new almanac on chimbley-piece. As soon as I saw there were two full moons this January I knew there'd be bother.' She left Jessie alone in the shop with her vividly powerful new dream, day-dreaming away under the shop gaslight. So it was that Throttlepenny found her.

He returned at seven. Always, after being out for some time, the old man, on returning, would squeeze himself into the gap between a cast-iron drainpipe and the shop next door, so that he could spy on Jessie. He did that now. He crouched in the cold shadows, his thin neck peering like an aggressive gander, his beady eyes sparkling with malice as he saw Jessie. She was standing by the shop fireplace warming herself, day-dreaming as likely as not, a smile on her face. The smile infuriated the old man. He thought the world a miserable place and hoped others did too. When it did not live up to his expectations he picked on Jessie. He suddenly leaped out of the gap and opened the shop door with a bang.

'Now I've caught ye!' This was an old trick, leaping in on Jessie. It made her jump. It made her look nervous and guilty. The old man at once began a grumbling tour of inspection round the shop. He began by turning down the gaslight, staring at poor Jessie as he did so, hissing between his yellow teeth as he turned the tap, as though he were in conversation with the hissing gas. Next he poured a little water from a cracked teapot he kept by the fire. This dampened the fire and saved coal. Now the fire hissed in sympathy with the turned-down gas and the miserly old man. Jessie stared, wide-eyed in the growing shadows. The shop was like a nestful of serpents. His beady sad old eyes darted hither and thither, hoping to find fault, ready to take a penny off her already pathetic wages.

'Ye careless lass. Ye've put new biscuits on top of old. If there's any weevils in old biscuits they'll rise up an' get in new ones. An' I'll have to sell 'em cheap. I canna afford to lose money.' With a flick of his wrist as fast as an adder's tongue, he reached for the ivory-handled butter knife and with the blunt side of the blade rapped Jessie's knuckles. She yelped in pain. Then he spotted some tiny grains of sugar that Jessie had spilled when listening to Aunty Lily's warnings.

'Come here, lass.' Jessie approached. 'What's that, then, spilled on counter?' Jessie bent to look at the star-like grains on the polished mahogany counter. As she bent, he whacked her bottom with the heavy brass coffee-bean scoop.

So, her mind full of dreams of revenge, the gas turned low like a wicked cat's eye, the old man and the girl tidied up. Jessie swept up, dreamed, polished the counter, hated, washed the butter knife, rubbed her stinging hands and aching bottom, put a guard round the fire, and pulled down the linen blinds over the windows. The old man counted the money, putting the little bags of gold into the tails of his ancient overcoat. He turned out the gas with a pop. Then they were out in the winter's night. He tried the shop door three times to check if it was locked. Then he walked away with a hiss and a growl, only to return and do the same thing another three times. Jessie, in the circle of gold on snow from the street gas lamp, dreamed her dreams and watched for devils. Then they were off. Jessie followed the old man, nursing her throbbing fingers in the bitterly cold January night. On Monday nights she went to the old man's house and cooked him a meal for sixpence. That meant that on Mondays she worked a fifteen-hour day, for she did not get home until eleven.

Now she followed him to his house for the last time. Under the frost-fiery shimmer of the stars, their boots crunched on the thin frosty snow. When they had walked for five minutes the old man suddenly stopped. 'Go back, will ye, and try the shop door?' No good arguing that she had seen him do it. She had to go back. Her legs ached. She tried the door dutifully. The dying red eye of the shop fire watched her try the door.

And she smiled as she went back to him, and she dreamed her dreams. She thought of the stone devils. Perhaps one would come and get him now. It was dark. The moon had not yet climbed over the distant East Moors. Because he had hit her, she would even help one. She had a weapon ready. She had the axe in her sackcloth bag on her arm. It was as keen and bright as the winter stars above. Yes, she thought, she'd hand over the axe. But only to frighten the horrible old man. She didn't really mean to kill him.

CHAPTER
[2]

JESSIE OBEDIENTLY followed the old man along the river path, as she had done so many times before. But tonight it was for the last time. She took her mind away from her aching legs and cold hands by a quick dream. She imagined the old man suddenly slipping on the icy river bank and giving a cry for help. She heard the cry as his body hit the star-streaked winter river. She heard his cries as he splashed about. Circular starlit splashes filled her mind, like the doilies her Aunty Betty at Derby stood her cakes on. 'Help me, Jessie my dear,' she heard him calling. She rushed to get a branch and hauled him out of the river. He stood there dripping and glistening like black silk. 'Jessie, I'll never be mean to thee again,' he said. She liked that dream and re-ran it several times, the pleasing phrase 'Jessie, my dear,' echoing in her mind. Then she dreamed of John sledging. Then her mind darkened with hatred and she dreamed of the stone devils, and her fingers felt the axe.

'Stop dawdling, ye idle little wench!' hissed the old man, his breath a cold trail in the night. 'I'll knock a penny off thy wages, I will.' Jessie's mind swarmed with stone devils taking him. His rasping voice disturbed the water birds on the river island. They made watery sounds of content. Jessie could see ripples of starshine where one or two took to the water. She heard a tin-trumpet call of a coot and she forgot her devilish dream. She loved birds, small animals and babies. Only the cold captivity with Throttlepenny made her seek comfort in dangerous dreams.

Their footsteps changed from a tapping on the path to a soft crunch as they left the path for Throttlepenny's house, which now loomed up and hid the southern stars. The house

9

stood in a small dark wood planted by Throttlepenny when he was a young man, forty years ago. Horse chestnuts and sycamores had grown as fast as the stealthy meanness had grown in Ezekiel Dobson's mind, blotting out all sunshine. He had built the house when he was an even younger man. A plaque of fine stone on the front of the house bore the words DOBSON HOUSE 1835. The letters were cut deep. The cost of the house had cut deep into the young newly-married Throttlepenny. As soon as it was built, Throttlepenny began to find ways of saving money to pay for the house, and the habit grew like a cancer into meanness. He had built the house for his young wife. But everything had gone wrong. He became cold and mean. His wife died. All light and warmth died in Throttlepenny from then on.

Jessie stopped her dreams as they crossed the tangled, frost-furred garden. Her Aunty Lily had told her that the house was haunted by the dead Mrs Dobson, that Mrs Dobson's sister had put a curse on the house when Mrs Dobson died. Jessie had thought about it often. Tonight she had the terrifying thought that the dead wife would glide into the kitchen and say, 'Jessie Smith . . . find me an axe . . . a knife . . . vengeance will be mine.' Jessie did not like that. It was somehow more frightening than the stone devils; perhaps, because she believed in ghosts, she felt there was more chance of it happening. Now they were deep in the shadows, and owls hooted and bubbled in the tree skeletons like black rivers against the stars. Jessie held on to her axe, praying now that no devil or ghost would rise up and ask her for it. Her dad had sharpened it for her last night and the smooth warm ashwood handle reminded her of him, so she clutched it tightly. They were right under the big dark house now, where the tall chimneys seemed to rake the stars, as though pulling them in to add to the old man's treasure. The old man unlocked the back door with a great deal of scraping, hissing and chain-rattling. As he peered at her his miserable suspicious eyes were full of the reflection of stars that he could no longer enjoy.

They were in. It felt colder in than out. 'Get busy. You know what to do.' He pushed her into the kitchen. Again she gripped her axe for comfort. She stumbled into the vast kitchen that had been designed to house cook, maids, footmen and butler by the rich young merchant shop-keeper, E. Dobson, Esq. Jessie groped for the matches on a dusty shelf, helped by the light of a great silver planet that shone through the window. She groped some more, hoping she was alone in the dark. She found a tallow dip in the bark on the shelf. The old miser had gone back to using rush dips, rushes dipped in mutton fat, just like his mother had used seventy years ago. Jessie struck a light, sighing with relief at the friendly spear of warm light. She lit a dip and put it in an iron clip. She felt cheered, but she dared not use more than one. She could hear the old man muttering somewhere deep in the still dark house.

She gripped her axe and opened a door into a room where wood was piled. She chopped a few sticks quickly. The axe was frighteningly sharp. Her dad had done it well. She had a daring dream as she gathered up the sticks. She would creep up on the old man and say, 'If you're not kind and good to me, I'll chop thee down the middle like a dry log.' And he would say, 'I'm sorry, Jessie my dear. Here's a sov to cheer thee up and buy thy ma and pa some good food.'

Still with this dream floating around, she dumped the sticks in the grate. Then she laid the axe on the table, smiling a secret smile to herself. She went over to a long low stone sink that had a tap. The tap gave Jessie great pleasure. It was the only tap in her life. At home they all shared a pump in the yard. The tap led to a huge lead cistern in the roof of Dobson House, that collected rain water. It had been a brilliant invention in 1835. Jessie filled a pail from it, half afraid of the slimy leaves, dead earwigs, bird-head skeletons and woodlice that sometimes came down in the water. Some days the pail contained swimming spiders and centipedes, so that it looked like a miniature circus. Today it was clear and cold, and she carried the pail over to the rusty range of ovens and boilers and began to fill the boilers. She did this many times. Then she lit the fire in the grate to heat the water. The old man had a bath after his Monday treat of a cooked meal.

That done, she opened a tiny parcel that contained one

lamb chop. His supper. The paper that wrapped the chop was stained with blood. Jessie put it by the axe on the table. Axe and bloody paper lay on the table like a warning of things to come.

Next she selected a pan with care. There were many shelves of once-fine copper pans, now green and black with age. She needed three pans, one for potatoes, one for the steamed pudding, one for the chop. She did not want to disturb the mice who nested in them. The baby mice, with tiny eyes like black stars in the rush light, always brought tears of love to her eyes. Neither did she wish to upset Horace Hairy Legs, as she called a giant spider who lived close by the frying pans. Jessie wished no creature any harm.

Glancing at the axe as though for comfort when the pans were on the fire, she went to set the table in the big cold dusty haunted dining room. The room shone silver with dust and frost as she lit the fire in the black marble grate. She set the table. The wood fire flared up and all was ready. Jessie paused and looked around her. She picked up a moth-eaten red velvet cushion and rubbed the expensive material against her face. The cushion had once been Mrs Dobson's. Jessie felt that by touching the cushion she would somehow placate the ghost of the dead woman. She was taking no chances while the axe was in the kitchen. Then she went into the kitchen to dish up the meal.

Throttlepenny liked her to stand behind his chair as he ate, like a real servant. It was a last luxury that he allowed himself once a week. Jessie stood behind him dreamily. She was now half asleep, and the dreams about the axe flowed through her mind with the vivid colours of night dreams. The grandfather clock struck ten o'clock. The last time the old man would hear it. Jessie had to keep blinking to stop the dreams taking over her mind completely. One trick was to keep looking at a big picture on the wall, called *VENUS AND CUPID* by William Etty. It was a big copy given to the old man by a grateful coffee merchant. It showed a lot of naughty ladies (Jessie thought) with nothing on. They were plump and white like cream cheese and had big bosoms. Jessie thought they were naughty, but nice. They stopped the dreams for the moment.

She made the coffee. A big pot. Then she stood and watched. She was the last person to see a glimpse of the man he had once been. It was a strange fact that the girl who was arrested for his murder was the last person to have any feelings for him.

He could not take out his gold and count it as he usually did after a meal—not with Jessie Smith there. So he took out a small mahogany chest of drawers, no bigger than a shoe box. This was his collection of birds' eggs. He pulled open the perfectly made silk-smooth drawers and revealed the soft pebble-coloured jewels of wild birds' eggs. All he had collected as a boy. His face softened in the candle-light. A new label was needed. He fetched ink. He sipped his coffee. He selected a crow quill, the very best for fine writing. His face relaxed as he wrote. LUSCINA MEGARHYNCHOS-NIGHTINGALE-MAY 1829. A rare bird in central Derbyshire. Jessie stared and stared. She saw in the wrinkled, dirty face the boy that he had once been. And she wished with all her heart that he would like her. She would have done anything at that moment to make him like her.

A movement at the window made them both turn. It was snowing outside, big solemn flakes. The happy interlude was gone for ever. The sixpence had to be given. The old man laid down his magnifying glass and slid out his gold glasses from their red velvet-lined case. Jessie noted dreamily that the velvet was the colour of the blood on the chop paper.

'I canna really afford it.'

'No, Mester Dobson,' murmured Jessie sleepily. She was nearly sleep-walking. Then to her last job. She had to fill a tin bath with water from the now hot boilers of water in the kitchen. Then she was pushed out.

Snow blew around her, soft and friendly after the hard human misery within the house. She picked some bright holly berries from the overgrown garden. Her tame robin back at home would like them tomorrow. She kept her eye open for the ghost of Mrs Dobson, but thinking of the hungry birds helped. Jessie knew what hunger felt like. Then she remembered the axe. Her dad's axe. She ran back to get it. The clouds above suddenly parted and the moon shone down on the garden. She reached the back door and peeped through the keyhole. The old man had removed his clothes and, standing with his feet in the hot bath, was crouched over the gold on the table, like a black and white hairy spider over its eggs. The axe was on the table by the blood-stained paper, as though waiting for something to happen. Jessie stared. Then she ran away giggling, her hands clasped tight round the berries she had gathered.

Fanny Gibbs and her mother saw her. They were returning from a tea and supper at a distant farmhouse further down the river. They would tell the Judge that they had seen Jessie creeping round the house, spying and waiting . . . Fanny Gibbs had been Jessie's worst enemy at school. They had both fancied John Mellor. Fanny had stayed on at school and was going to become a pupil teacher. A year ago she would have yelled to Jessie, 'Nosey Nellie . . . Keyhole Kate!' Now that she was going to be a teacher she said nothing, but looked at her mother in the moonlight and made a face of disgust.

Home at last. Away from the doomed man. Her mam was nodding by the fire, her dad asleep. They always waited for her. The newest baby lay asleep before the fire in a drawer. Jessie stuffed herself with bread and cheese from the table, kissed her mother awake, hugged her dad, and then ran upstairs with a candle and a warm brick wrapped in cloth. She kissed her brothers, asleep in the big bed, and tenderly arranged the old coats and blankets over them. Then she climbed the ladder to her loft. This was a tiny room under the slates, with a square of glass on a hinge, that let in the sun or the moon, a great deal of cold, and razor-edged draughts. But it was Jessie's palace. Hers. It was private. Nobody ever came up. Here were all the treasures she had in the world.

There was a tap at the moonlit glass. It was Smut the cat. She let him in, admiring his sapphire and diamond paw prints across the snow-covered slates. She hugged him

14

to her, which he allowed because he wanted to sleep warm that night on her mattress. He sat by the warm brick on the mattress, his tail twitching with irritation, for Jessie was not getting into bed. She was doing something else. Cats do not like to be kept waiting.

At school, when the Headmaster, Marmaduke Middlemas, caned children, he wrote their names in a big black leather book with PUNISHMENT BOOK written on the front in gold leaf. It was the Punishment Book that Jessie remembered most about her seven years at school. Perhaps that was why she dreamed so much of punishing Throttlepenny. She had wanted a Punishment Book too. So she had stolen a Cash Book from Throttlepenny's shop. It was a nice book, striped blue and brown and white, like winter mist caught in a ploughed field under a blue sky. In this book she wrote down her punishments for Throttlepenny, just like the teachers had at school. She copied them carefully. Her Punishment Book looked like this.

NAME	MISDEED	PUNISHMENT
E. Dobson	Smacking my bum	A kick up his bum
E. Dobson	For saying bad words when I spilled sugar	One slug with his onions on his chop next Monday
E. Dobson	For hurting my knuckles with a knife	A level spoonful of mouse droppings in his coffee
E. Dobson	For nipping my bum	An axe waved under his nose till he says sorry
E. Dobson	For ticking me for weighing cheese slowly	A push in the river, a nail in his boot and another warning with the axe

Jessie wrote in the book with care. She did not know that when she left the axe on the table, and Fanny Gibbs saw her peeping through the door, she had left the world of dreams far behind her. They would use this Punishment Book too against her. Dreams are important but shadowy. The Punishment Book was real evidence.

CHAPTER
[3]

THE NEXT day, the day of the murder, was a busy one in the shop. Yesterday had been a day of dreams. They played their part in the mystery to come. But today was the day when people collected evidence against Jessie. Dreams, however powerful, cannot be seen. Today Jessie did things that people saw and told against her. It had begun last night when Fanny Gibbs had seen her spying through the keyhole, and with the writing she had done in the Punishment Book.

Jessie was up when the stars still shone. It was six o'clock. She came down her ladder sleepily to her mam and dad. Her mam's hair was stretched out on the striped pillow. She lit a fragment of stolen candle for her mam on a saucer, to wake her gently. She had stolen the candle as a punishment against Throttlepenny. The baby was mewing like a kitten. She picked him up lovingly and warmed milk for him. She loved his soft skin and the milky smells. Her eyes softened with love for him, as outside the stars began to soften as the dawn came.

'You buzz our Tom,' she said to the baby. She held him down to change him, playing peek-a-boo to him as she did so. He gurgled and cooed. The door was pushed open irritably and Smut walked in, talking to her in that curious half-purred cat talk that cats use for people who worship them. Then there was a light tap at the window. It was the robin come for his crumbs. Everybody wanted her. All except Throttlepenny. She talked to the robin, admiring the red breast and the frosty sunrise behind him. Inside her a flame of love and happiness burned too.

Looking after everybody made her five minutes late at

17

the shop. Throttlepenny seized her and shook her, shaking out the flame of love and joy. He nipped her bottom as she pulled up the blinds. They were busy that last morning. Then the afternoon began to tick away, and his spoiled life with it.

Jessie ate the lunch of bread and fat bacon she had brought at two o'clock, eating it on a barrel in the yard and sharing it with the sparrows. She sat there too long and he crept up behind her and made her jump. 'Time tha was in shop.' Jessie's mild eyes blazed. He had startled a sparrow with a broken wing. When they were back in the shop and as he was muttering over a sack of dried peas, she aimed her boot at his thin mean bottom and kicked at it, narrowly missing the withered object by a hair's breadth. It was a trick she had perfected over the last weeks. She did not see the customer in the shop. It was Mrs Mellor, her sweetheart's mother.

'You'll do that once too often my girl,' she said. She did not like Jessie. Now her John was working at the Castle, she did not want him mixing with the likes of Jessie. Later Mrs Mellor told the Judge about what she had seen.

Jessie saw Throttlepenny amble over the yard to the privy. She was weighing crumbly, salty fragrant Cheshire cheese. Her mouth had been watering for the last fifteen minutes, so she ate a tiny crumb. Then she looked up. He was looming over her, white apron over stove-pipe trousers. He smacked her over her ears twice. So when he was fidgeting over some expensive vanilla pods he sold for flavouring, she pretended to stab him with a bacon knife.

'Jessie my love, there's many a true thought acted in jest. Don't even think such dark thoughts. You'm too grand a lass for that.' Old Mrs Walton was in the shop. Jessie hadn't seen her. But old Mrs Walton was a friend. She did not tell.

But the next customer did. It was Miss Clara Stardrop, the proud Housekeeper from Blackdon Castle. Her face was as cold as a dusty icicle in its black bonnet. She bought and ordered a great deal of food. Throttlepenny himself carried out the more important parcels that she was taking back herself to the Castle. It was good for trade for people to see her buying his groceries. Jessie watched them, wide eyed. Here was the chance she had been waiting for. In Throttlepenny's store room were some mice he'd trapped in a cage. Soon he would kill them. They had moth-grey bodies as soft as rainclouds. Jessie opened the trap, talking to the mice as they whisked free. Then back into the room walked Throttlepenny and Miss Stardrop to smell some new tea that the Duchess might like back at the Castle. They raged over her head. Miss Stardrop looked at her as though she had crawled out of a maggot-hole. 'Girls cannot be trusted these days . . . no thought for anyone save themselves . . . the new school has taught her nothing . . . good-for-nothing slut.' Miss Stardrop repeated this to the Judge.

Then Throttlepenny made her reset the trap. Jessie had never been so angry. She was too angry to dream properly. She watched through narrow eyes the Head Gardener from the Castle come in, with a basket of snowdrops tied up in bunches with ivy leaves around them. Tucker, the gardener, took them from the Castle and Throttlepenny sold them for a penny a bunch. The two old men split the profits. Throttlepenny always took flowers to his wife's grave. 'And I hope one of them stone devils gets thee and splits thy ugly head right down the middle,' thought Jessie. 'And I hope it happens this very night.' The power of her wish made her rock on her heels. She was still rocking when the hated Fanny Gibbs sailed into the shop. The two girls glared at each other. Both fancied John Mellor. Jessie knew all about bad luck and always had the feeling that one day John would leave her for the clever-clogs Fanny. Fanny had all that Jessie did not have. She had a rich mother and father. She was well fed. She had been good at sewing and sums and writing. She had all that Jessie did not have . . . except a warm heart and John Mellor.

Fanny was flouncing about in a purple cloak because her family were mourning for her grandfather. The colour suited Fanny and she knew it. She had a black sable muff. Throttlepenny fussed round her, slobbering at her beauty. 'Dirty old devil,' thought Jessie, wildly jealous nevertheless. She watched, still rocking with hatred at the old man, as he pinned a bunch of snowdrops on to Fanny's bosom. Then he went to get a ham her mother had ordered.

'Put your eyes back in your head, Jessie Smith,' said Fanny, in what she thought was the right voice for someone who was a pupil teacher. 'Get on with what Mr Dobson pays you for. And that's not staring at my new muff or looking through keyholes.' Fanny had always been cruel. She turned on her dazzling smile as Throttlepenny returned.

'I'm having a Twelfth Night Party tonight, Mr Dobson. All my friends are coming. Mother is letting us have the sitting room to ourselves.' She turned to Jessie. 'I expect you are going sledging tonight in the churchyard with John?' Jessie nodded. She had been so angry she had forgotten that. She'd be in the churchyard when Throttlepenny was there! She'd call out for a stone devil to come and get Throttlepenny, then it would—'Good,' said Fanny. 'When you've finished sledging I'll ask John to come to my party. He'll be ready for some delicious warming food.'

Fanny began to order. As she did so, Jessie's hatred and imaginings could almost be felt.

Heart-shaped biscuits with whorls of sugar icing were bought. Sugar plums were wrapped up and round wooden boxes of Turkish Delight. Round trays of dried fruit, apricots, figs and dates were bought. Fruits preserved in sugar were carefully paid for. Orange, lemon and cherry jellies in fancy jars. Marzipan fruits. Pounds of sugared biscuits. Jessie was so overcome with dreams and jealousy that she stole a bunch of snowdrops when she thought they were both not looking. She would pin the snowdrops to her shawl when they were sledging tonight. But Fanny's darting school-mistress eyes saw her. She said nothing then, but it was mentioned in Court.

John Mellor walked along the turnpike road, chalked with frost and snow, on his way to Lambton. It was his afternoon off from the stables. He was going home. Then he and Jessie would go to the steep churchyard and sledge. John had heard about the stone devils when he had been

sent to the farrier in Lambton yesterday. A horse had been
sick and they needed some special advice. The farrier was a
superstitious old man and collected stories like that. John
was not a dreamer like Jessie but he thought a lot. He
thought that perhaps one of these devils might get
Throttlepenny in the churchyard when he went to his wife's
grave. Jessie and he might see a devil getting Throttlepenny
tonight. He hated Throttlepenny as much as he loved
Jessie.

Loved Jessie? Two years ago at school he had teased and
pinched and bullied her. A year ago they had seen a ghost
together in the woods to the east of the town. And suddenly
he had wanted to protect her. He was pulled to the warmth
that Jessie gave out. He thought a lot about her now. He
made up stories in his head where he imagined himself
rescuing Jessie from great danger . . . even getting rid of
that mean old man Ezekiel Dobson for her. Jessie made him
feel all right. She gave him feelings like he felt for the soft
warmth of the stable kittens.

John reached Throttlepenny's shop at six o'clock. He
wanted some muffins and butter to have for tea with his
mother. Then he would collect Jessie and they would go to
the churchyard. He asked for a pound of butter in the shop
and passed her a sweet. It was a pink round violet-scented
heart and written on it in tiny writing were the words
WILL YOU BE MINE? Jessie had some in her pocket and
giggling, with her back to the old man, she passed John a
sweet that said WHEN PIGS FLY!

'I'll come for thee at eight, Jessie,' said John. He went.
Jessie glowed all over with happiness. He was back at eight
o'clock, standing under the gas lamp outside the shop,
snowflakes caught in his short cropped hair that shone gold
under the gaslight. Jessie stared out at him as though at a
vision, and had to be pinched by Throttlepenny to come
out of her trance.

Throttlepenny made his last hour on earth as difficult as
possible for himself. Sometimes Jessie thought the old man
had eyes in his bum with glasses on, as he seemed to see so
much that went on behind his back. 'Ye canna go yet. Ye
spilled some butterbeans this morning. Get 'em out from

21

behind the sack. Go on. And there's still some coffee beans left in coffee mill. Put 'em back in the tin.' So she had to find three dusty beans no good to anybody behind the sack, and unscrew the coffee grinder. The old man began to count his gold.

John waited patiently outside, stamping his boots and blowing on his hands. He watched a navvyman swaggering down the street. Railways were still being built in Derbyshire and there was good money to be had building them. John, in his drab jacket and boots and brown cords, admired the navvy. His mouth opened a little as the navvyman paused outside the shop door and looked in. John took in all the details of the man. Brown velveteen jacket with pearl buttons. A moleskin waistcoat. The navvy's cord breeches, of finer quality than John's, were tucked into high leather boots. There was a billycan strapped to the man's leg above the high-laced working boots. There was a slab of snow on his peaked cap. The man had walked some distance. He felt in his pocket and jingled some money then banged on the door of the shop.

Inside, Throttlepenny was undecided. He did not like opening up the shop once it was shut. On the other hand, it would delay Jessie further. He let the man in. The navvyman stared long and hard at the gold Throttlepenny had laid out in reverent piles along the counter, as Throttlepenny got him a jar of pickles, two pounds of cheese and a plum cake. Jessie stared outside at John, dreaming her dreams.

'Work short?' asked Throttlepenny, eager to delay Jessie and enquire into the misfortunes of others.

'I'm on my way to the High Peak line,' said the navvy. 'They're rebuilding it.' His eyes strayed to the gold and he looked at the old man keenly. Then he was through the shop door, ducking his head as he went, for he was a giant of a man. Then Throttlepenny had to let Jessie go too and she was out, smiling at John, pinning the stolen snowdrops to her ragged shawl and trembling with joy and excitement.

'I'll kill that old devil one day,' said John.

So they all went to the churchyard, the scene of the murder. Jessie and John hand in hand now, John narrowing his eyes to watch the navvy walking ahead, still admiring his clothes. Soon after, Throttlepenny locked the shop up and went to the churchyard to put snowdrops on his wife's grave.

Throttlepenny had minutes to live. Soon Jessie, John and the navvy would be caught up in a devilish scene by the church.

CHAPTER
[4]

JESSIE'S WAS a warm hatred for Throttlepenny. It glowed in her like a red-hot cinder bringing a flush to her cheeks, a twinkle to her eye and a smile to her lips. But a glowing cinder can start a blazing fire. It was quite different from the candle-flame of love she felt for John, her parents, her brothers and the animals.

There was someone else who hated Throttlepenny more than Jessie did. That was Emma Briddon. Her hatred for Throttlepenny was ice cold. A frozen withering hatred that would never thaw. It kept her mouth a frozen line, her nose blue, her eyes pale and her soul like cold stone. For Emma's beloved younger sister had married Throttlepenny fifty years ago, and when she died Emma had blamed Throttle-penny's mean ways for her death. She had grieved for her sister ever since.

Every Tuesday night, including this one, sun, moon, rain, storm, gale, Emma walked down from the village of One Ash to the churchyard. It had been on a Tuesday that her sister had died.

She was there tonight at the scene of the murder. Her black cloak, bought for the funeral over fifty years ago, flapped in the keen east wind. Her face was narrow and the skin seemed only a thin covering over her skull. She stood in the cold moonlight that so matched her grief. The moon shone on her white face making it glow like white bone. She had taken off the black kid gloves and her fingernails shone like cold pearls. After standing by the grave, she would often walk around the gravestones, weeping for her lost sister. She began to walk about that night. The churchyard was littered with boulders and fragments of carvings and

24

masonry. The church of All Saints had been severely shaken by earth tremors some months before, and the builders had not yet begun to restore it. But tonight Emma did not cry as she picked her way round the tombstones and waited in the shadows. She laughed. The laughter was as uncanny and out of place as distant thunder on a frosty winter's night. Emma's sinister laughter was an eerie prelude to Throttlepenny's murder.

The railway navvy was keeping out of sight as well. He wanted to eat his supper and sleep in the big church porch. The porch had some rush matting on the floor where he could eat his cheese and pickles. He had found it out earlier in the day. Sleeping there would be better than going to the Lambton Union Workhouse and being put in a cell for the night. He would have to find work tomorrow. He had heard there might be work on the High Peak line. He had also heard that work might not start until March or April. If there was no work, he did not know what he was going to do. His pocketful of money would not last long. Now he leaned up against a small stump of ancient stone, munching onions. His face was like a black and white, watchful engraving—teeth gleaming in the moonlight, white skin, black eyes and black moustache—as he waited to see that nobody would watch him enter the church.

Unaware of his coming death, Ezekiel Dobson, known as Throttlepenny, entered the graveyard by the south gate and walked slowly and painfully, a crooked shadow in the moonlight, to the grave of the woman he once loved as warmly as Jessie now loved John.

CHAPTER
[5]

JESSIE JUMPED for joy. Stars in her eyes twinkled like the ones caught in the fine lime trees that bordered the big steep churchyard. Suddenly the church grounds were full of children. It was well known that Dr Ball, the Vicar, went for his supper at half-past eight, and the older children in the town nagged unceasingly at their parents to be allowed some sledging before bedtime. Dr Ball would not allow sledging in the churchyard, but as soon as he had vanished children appeared as if from nowhere. It was a perfect sledge run. In olden times, the main road had gone through the churchyard. That was now closed off. The run was the church path, and it gave the children a quarter of a mile of downhill sledging, beginning at the west gate and ending at the east wall by the dangerous iron gates. The danger only added excitement. A crash into the iron gates at high speed could have killed a child. Likewise a collision with a gravestone ... It all added to the pleasure. And the churchyard was said to be haunted ... It was a perfect spot.

The navvy swore when he saw the children. He stepped back into the shadows. Emma Briddon did the same, laughing softly in the moon shadows. Throttlepenny stood humbly by his wife's grave. He often walked about around the grave for many minutes, restless and miserable.

But Jessie jumped for joy. Sam Walton had brought his big sledge. It had belonged to his dad and his five brothers. It was very heavy, very big and very, very fast. Jessie could sit on it with Sam and John, and wind her arms tight around John.

They sat on the big sledge and were away. The stars

26

streamed by, Jessie screamed and screamed. The grave-
stones seemed to bow and leap as they sped by Throttlepenny and, like Jessie's dreams, they left the old man far
behind. Every leaping shadow was a devil to get Throttlepenny in Jessie's excited mind. Faster and faster, and the
world spun round them until Sam yelled, 'Jump for it!' and
they rolled off into the soft snow before the iron gates. Jessie
laughed and laughed, her face in the snow and her
snowdrops ruined. She rolled over and over and stood up,
weak and wobbly with extreme pleasure.

She looked up. And there was Fanny Gibbs. As soon as
she saw Jessie, she began to speak to John.

'It's my Twelfth Night Party tonight, John. There's lots
of lovely things to eat and drink, and we're going to play
Snapdragon. It would be lovely if you could come.' It was a
pretty, prepared speech. Jessie sadly picked at the bunch of
squashed snowdrops fastened to her shawl. Of course she
was not included in the invitation. John dusted some
powdery snow off his corduroys.

'Nay. Not tonight, Fan, thanks. I've better things to do.'

For Jessie the world danced. The Plough high over the
northern moors seemed to whirl in the sky. The carved
stone devils on the tower seemed to move and laugh, and
the Dog Star over the distant Castle winked at her. She
clasped her hands together as Fanny swirled away in her
purple cloak. Fanny had put on her new tam-o'-shanter
cap, a bright red tartan with a silver and amethyst thistle, a
Christmas present. She was bitterly disappointed. She
would get Jessie Smith for that.

But down down down they went on their sledge, again
and again, Sam's, Jessie's and John's whole bodies tingling
with excitement and warmth from lugging the heavy sledge
up to the top of the churchyard. They paused for breath
after the seventh breathtaking journey, only to hear in the
distance the fast tap of the footsteps of Dr Ball, tapping
irritably out along the path to the Vicarage. He was intent
on trouble. Sam sped away on his sledge laughing, and
shouting to the whole of the churchyard, 'Canon Ball's
coming!'

At once children sledging on tin trays, old mats, wooden

sledges ran for home whooping with glee. It had been good while it lasted. Now it was time for home and bed. John did not want to go home yet and neither did Jessie. John ran off laughing to the church porch, shouting to Jessie to follow. Jessie was too weak with excitement, happiness and hunger to follow him so she hid giggling behind a tombstone.

Emma Briddon in the shadows curtsied to Dr Ball, but he was so intent on stopping the sledging that he did not see her. The navvy swore viciously again when he saw the Vicar. He wanted to rest in the porch.

Dr Ball stood panting in the cold air, gathering his cloak around him. If only he could catch one culprit. Then he saw a movement in the porch of the church. A boy, he shouldn't wonder. He strode after him purposefully. Throttlepenny bent down to lay the bunch of snowdrops on his wife's grave. His life was drawing to its close.

CHAPTER
[6]

JOHN IN the porch had no fear of Dr Ball. He could outrun the Vicar any day. He only laughed the more when he heard Dr Ball coming towards him, and he entered the church. He at once sneezed from the thick coke fumes, and he heard Dr Ball's fidgeting footsteps quicken behind him. He grinned. If Dr Ball wanted to play at hide and seek in the church, he knew who would win. His eyes soon became accustomed to the darkness. Two big candles burned at the east end of the church and moonlight filtered through every window. John knew where he would hide. He would go up into the tower where there was a library. He had once been the bellows boy, pumping air into the organ for Sunday services. He knew the church well.

Dr Ball, finding no trace of a boy hiding, began to wonder if he had imagined one. While he was in the church, he decided to fetch a book from the parish chest in the tower. John, hearing him coming up the winding stairs, swore. This meant he would have to go higher. In the wall of the library was a small door that led to a ladder, which went up to the bells, then out on to the battlements below the spire. John grinned. He'd go up and wave to Jessie, or look down anyway. He climbed up the ladder. Dr Ball would never follow him here. He peeped in at the clock works, grey and white with the dust of time and frost. Then up and up to the bells. It was by the bells that a wave of fear shivered through his body. Something was wrong. There was an air of expectancy like there had been in the woods that day, when he and Jessie had seen ... He shook his head. The bells were almost menacing him. The great tenor bell loomed up in the starlight. A wedge of moonlight fell on the rim. John could read words carved in the huge bell:

> Possessed of deep & sonorous tone
> This belfry King sits on his throne.

John suddenly had the strange feeling that the whole of the big church was alive and waiting. He remembered the farrier's story of the stone devils. He was glad to step out on to the narrow balcony below the spire and get his breath in the moonlight. There was a stone wall on the balcony of the tower below the spire and John felt safe. But the creepy feeling that the church was alive and watching him did not go, as he had expected it to when he emerged into the brilliant snow and moonlight. In fact the cold air was almost heavy with menace.

He stood on the toes of his boots and looked over the wall. He could not see below him, as he had hoped. There was a slab of black moon shadow and webs of shadow from the trees, and chequer-board shadows from the grave-stones. He leaned out dangerously far, resting his hand on a stone devil's head that drained the water from the spire.

Suddenly the stars seemed to flash light at him as though they had all come together for a moment, uniting their light in a wave of star fire. His body went ice cold and his head spun in a violent dizziness. He rocked dangerously. Then he heard a laugh, wild and unearthly. In the sharp and expectant frosty air, it seemed to John that it came from the hideous stone devil that he rested against. He felt for a few seconds as if some invisible hand were trying to pull him into the air and a voice were whispering to him that he could leap into the silvered air and soar above the loop of the moonlit river far below the town. He clung to the stonework, shaking with fear and horror. As the wild laughter died, so did his desire to jump, and the giddy feeling left his body. Now he could see Throttlepenny directly under him, kneeling on the white mound of the grave. But he could not see the navvy, or Emma Briddon, or Jessie.

He looked at the stone devil again, the gargoyle, one of

Aunty Lily's stone devils. It had a wicked pointed face, half-human, half-catlike. There had once been curved horns on its head, but nine hundred years had almost weathered them away. Around the long slender neck of the carving were the coils of a snake or great worm. John moved instinctively away. He knew the power of the old Lambton legends. But his hand seemed unable to leave the creature. It was glued to the thin sheet of ice that glossed the devil. His hand seemed stuck to the creature's head. All through Christmas and the twelve days after it, the gargoyle had dribbled water that slowly changed to ice. John could not see it, but under his hand, hanging from the mouth, there were two fang-like icicles. John stood, half tranced, while he felt the stone and ice draining the warmth from his hand and body.

A drop of water from the heat of John's hand trickled down the ice fang and fell to the ground, a hundred feet below. Then another. And another. Drip . . . drip . . . drip . . . a rhythm like the last heartbeats of Throttlepenny.

John put the fingers of his other hand into his mouth to imitate an owl, to amuse Jessie as well as to scare Throttlepenny. He leaned more heavily on the gargoyle. The two fangs of ice suddenly cracked and fell to earth like twin shooting stars. From the inside of the devil's mouth, a lump of frost-cracked stone fell after the icicles. It was a serpent's tongue from the inside of the gargoyle. John stepped back in case anybody should look up after it fell. He quickly began climbing down the ladder. As he put his boot on the first rung, he heard the devilish laugh again echo up through the frosty air. He would get down, and fast.

Dr Ball had long given up the chase. He had moved to the altar and said an evening prayer. As he crossed the moonlit church to find the brass candle snuffers, he heard a faint laugh. No matter. Children again. He would talk to the Headmaster tomorrow and see that the children were caned. He was hungry now.

Ezekiel Dobson clutched his head. The falling stone had hit him. It was a painful and cruel blow for an old man, and for a moment he felt a searing pain. Then it went. A warmth passed through his body and suddenly the warm scenes of his whole life passed through his mind's eye. He was suddenly young again, back in 1815. He was with his best friend, Abel Walton, now dead, and they were watching the townsfolk build a huge bonfire to celebrate the Battle of Waterloo . . . or were Abel and himself going bird-nesting up on the high lane to Chesterfield, for he could hear the tinkling of packhorse pony bells . . . or was it a blackbird singing? . . . No, he was swimming in the river when he was twelve, with Abel, you could hear the sound of the great waterfall, all green and silver below Lambton Bridge . . . No, the sound was church bells and he was holding the hand of his lovely wife, Letitia, on their wedding day . . . the sound of bells crashed in his ears on that lovely April day in 1831, and the warm river became warm tears on his cheek. But he saw no more of his life, for a second and violent blow made him unconscious. He saw and knew no more. The old man, who had once been as young and happy as Jessie, lay dead, sprawled across the grave. His body lay in the cold snow, out of sight of anyone but the inquisitive, on that cold January night. The Throttlepenny Murder had taken place.

CHAPTER
[7]

JESSIE, LIKE John, had heard the strange echoing laugh, as she hid close by Throttlepenny before he was murdered. She had at first looked behind her, for she was certain that the horrid laughter came from the shadows under the church wall, as though somebody were hiding there. But the sound seemed to echo, twist and coil in the frosty night air around the church, until she thought it was coming from above her. At once she thought of Aunty Lily. Had her dream come true? Like a lot of people, Jessie found that when a dream became reality she did not like it. Then she smiled a warm smile. It was John up there, trying to make her laugh, and frighten Throttlepenny. She waved. He did not see her. Then to her utmost amazement, she saw a shining flash of dull glassy silver as the stone tongue fell from the devil's mouth. She saw it hit the old man on his head, and she put her hand over her mouth in a quick movement of shared agony with him. It was not a really big lump of stone, but enough to hurt an old man badly. The old man, however, though he swayed, did not appear badly hurt. But he was hurt, she could see that. She looked up again. There was no sign of John.

In a sudden flash of understanding Jessie saw, or thought she saw, what had happened. John had dropped a stone to make Throttlepenny jump. He had done it for her, to make her laugh when the old man jumped out of his skin. But the trick had gone wrong. The stone had hit the old man. She now forgot the old man, who was swaying a little with a happy look on his face. She thought of one person only, and that was John. If ever anybody found out what John had

33

done, there would be the most terrible trouble and John would probably lose his job. She must help John. Hardly noticing the old man, who now had his eyes shut anyway, Jessie darted forward and picked up the lump of stone that looked so similar to many other bits around the churchyard. There were piles all around, left over from the curious earth tremors of 1883. Stones and carvings had fallen off all round the church.

She would take the stone away. Nobody would ever know what had happened if she took the bit of stone with her. If this bit were found near the old man, he might remember what had happened and tell Dr Ball. There were no other bits really near, so Dr Ball and Throttlepenny would realize somebody had dropped it from above. So thought Jessie in her wild panic to save John from trouble. She should have tossed the lump of stone on to a distant pile of other stones. But she did not. She thought all this out in a matter of seconds and then she was running away with the stone held in her hand, and the old man was still swaying. She must get away quickly. Nobody must ever know what had happened. Never. John must not get in bother.

She ran wildly down the icy path with the stone in her hand. She thought she heard a laugh. Then she heard a strange sound. She hoped the old man had not fallen down, but she dared not go back. She was full of panic for John. She must save him from trouble. Out she ran through the east gate, the iron gates clanging dismally behind her. Her boots rang on the icy cobbles of Blackdon Square, deserted in the moonlight. She nearly lost her balance and waved the stone to correct herself. Then she fell on the cold ice that had little peaks of blue frost fire, like tiny volcanoes. The ice ripped her stockings and her flesh but she felt nothing. She must hide the stone and save John from any trouble.

Out of the south gate ran the navvy. He was shaking all over. Nobody saw him. As he ran, he made little sobbing noises and a great deal of money jingled in the deep wide pockets of his corduroy breeches. His cap was pulled down over his wild eyes. He looked as if he had seen a ghost or devil. He ran for his life down the deserted Derby Road that led to the woods and the Castle.

Out of the west gate walked Emma Briddon. She was walking back to One Ash, as she often did. She was dusting her black gloves as she walked, a habit of hers after she had visited the churchyard, as though she were ridding her hands of something. Nobody saw her. If they had, they would have thought no more about it. She had been coming for fifty years. She walked away up the winding hill road, like a grim shadowy ship of death upon a frozen silver river.

Dr Ball had lingered in the church. The sight of the moonlight through the stained glass thrilled him. It fell on the old stone floor like a dim silken coat of many colours. Then he saw the night sky through one of the plain glass windows, a deep blue sea with ivory boats of dim clouds sailing by. He held up his arms to the beauty of the church, the night sky and God's glory. A planet, like a fragment of broken mirror, shimmered above a cloud. 'Oh God, maker of all things and judge of all men, I thank thee for the wonder and glory of the heavens and thy inestimable handiwork . . . ' prayed Dr Ball, wrapped in wonder and a warm black cloak. He prayed for many minutes and heard nothing but the sound of his own voice, and saw nothing but the glory of God. Then he went out of the church, tapping along the path as quickly as he had come. He was ready for a bottle of port and a light supper. He thought the churchyard was empty of people, and thought how beautiful it looked in the moonlight.

John had hidden on the old staircase, waiting for him to go. The walls were thick and protective. He heard nothing but the drone of Dr Ball. He waited for him to go out of the church and after a few minutes he went out into the seemingly deserted churchyard. Dr Ball had long gone through the private gate to the Vicarage, the navvy had gone out of the south gate, and Emma Briddon out of the west gate. Jessie was now at home with the stone tongue. So John thought he was alone. He could not see the battered and pathetic body of Ezekiel Dobson sprawled over the grave of his wife. John laughed out loud with the sheer pleasure of the adventure. They had had a good sledge and a game with Dr Ball. Whistling and laughing, not noticing how the sound spiralled and echoed round the church, John walked towards the south gate. It was time to get back to Blackdon Castle where he worked.

He began to run and slide down the two miles of long straight snow-silent road that led to the Castle. Up above him owls hooted in the snow-filled twigs, vaulted under the sky, curved and traced like the stone carving in the church where he had been hiding. Now and again he leaped high to shake snow off a low branch, then dived forward to miss the tiny snowstorm he had made. Happy, without a care in the world, he reached the stables of Blackdon Castle, as long as a village street. Whistling under his breath, he made a tour round the warm stables to check on the fine horses that were in his care that night.

CHAPTER
[8]

THE GAS LAMPS were turned up. The coal fire blazed away in its red and green tiled fireplace. Golden gaslight and firelight made the lace-trimmed chair backs golden. On the table, resting on a thick red-plush cloth, was a large willow-patterned meat dish, solid with raisins. By its side stood a bottle of brandy. Round the table sat the friends of Fanny Gibbs. At the head of the table, undisputed queen of them all, was Fanny. This was her party. All the girls envied her, particularly her best friend Dolly. But Fanny was not happy. She wanted John to be at her party. She could not get him out of her mind. She wanted him here, now. And all he had wanted to do was sledge up and down with that mucky Jessie Smith. Now her mother and father, or her mama and papa, as she had lately begun to call them, were standing by the table ready to begin the Twelfth Night party game Snapdragon. But Fanny was not interested in it any more. She wanted John.

'I won't be a minute, mama,' she suddenly said. 'I think I left the gas lamp on upstairs.' Before her adoring parents could say anything, she sailed across the room, conscious of her girl-friends' admiring gaze on her. But she did not go upstairs. She went downstairs to the basement kitchen and grabbed a large hot mincepie as big as a saucer, her mother's speciality. She grabbed a clean white napkin, starched and crackling, with a 'G' embroidered in the corner, and put the pie in it. Then she let herself out of the back door into the moonlight, and began to run down the hill towards the church.

She felt very daring as she clutched the pie to her. She had no cloak on. She was going to take John a hot pie as he sledged. She would let him see her new party dress of expensive holly green velvet that showed off her blonde ringlets very well. He would also see the moonstone on a real gold chain round her neck, and the matching moonstone drops in her ears. She would show that little baggage Jessie Smith. She felt she was having a real adventure. This was better than being with her boring friends in the front sitting room.

She began to slip and slide, and her balance nearly went. The road from her house led down to the north gate of the churchyard before plunging downhill into Blackdon Square. Fanny had to grab one of the iron railings by the north gate to steady herself. She had on her new patent leather boots with the pearl buttons, again for John's glance. As she steadied herself by the gate, she looked up. She almost cried out as she saw a figure on the battlements below the spire. At first, for a fleeting moment, she thought it was one of the stone creatures the children had been talking about in school. But Fanny was not a believer in ghosts. She was also blessed with excellent long sight. She saw quickly that it was John up there.

But what was he doing? She stared up at the tower and the spire. Even at this distance she felt quite overcome by him, and she watched his every move. She saw him lean over in the moonlight. He seemed to be there for quite a time. The moonlight silvered his shabby clothes and his short hair. Fanny began to think he looked like a carving himself . . . a Greek one, perhaps. She had been learning about Greek statues and sculpture from Mr Middlemas, her headmaster. Then John seemed to drop a stone.

Fanny was only thirteen, and not as grown up as she thought. The budding teacher in her could see that John had done something dangerous. But she gave a low rich giggle. Perhaps the stone would hit Jessie Smith on her dirty nit-filled hair. She giggled again. Then she stopped. She did not know what to do. She stood there for some time, clutching the pie to her to warm herself. She could see into the church. The north gate was closer to the church than any of the other gates, and blocked Fanny's view of any other events. She could see in the church the figure of Dr

Ball. She was scared of Dr Ball. He came to the school to watch her teaching religious lessons. He would frown if he saw her without a cloak and hat. John had disappeared.

She tossed her head. Well, let him. John and Jessie were obviously playing some silly game. She thought she heard footsteps, and somebody coughing. Then she thought she heard a laugh. She did not like the sound of that laugh. It sounded almost inhuman. She began to walk back up the hill, her boots tapping on the ice.

Fanny glanced down the steep road that led to Blackdon Square. She stopped and stared. There was Jessie Smith, running for her life. Fanny could see she was carrying something. Fanny's keen eyes stared. She saw Jessie fall. It looked like a lump of stone or ice she was carrying. Fanny did not giggle when she saw Jessie fall. She was too angry. They were playing some silly game, dropping snowballs or stones from the tower and then running away.

There were tears in Fanny's eyes as she let herself into the kitchen, then returned to her party.

'Fan, my dear, what a time you've been. Your company is quite ready for the game. You must not keep guests waiting.' Fanny was glad her mother had turned down the gas, which hid her tears. Why, why, why did big handsome John want to play with mucky, smelly, ragged Jessie Smith.

Her father poured the brandy on the big dish of raisins and lit the brandy. A cool silent blue flame danced and flickered over the dish. The faces of the girls became blue and white. The darting swaying flames brought out the anger, jealousy and cruelty in Fanny's face. Over and over in her mind she saw the scene in the churchyard. And each time she saw it, the stone that John dropped got bigger, and the object that Jessie was running with, probably also a stone, got bigger too.

Her guests reached out to try and grab a flaming brandy-soaked raisin with screams of delight. The flames burned Fanny, and the stone that John had dropped grew bigger still in her mind's eye. Her father spoke the old Snapdragon rhyme with relish. Fanny could almost have screamed as he said it, she wanted John so much . . .

39

Here he comes with flaming bowl
Don't be mean to take his toll
Snip! Snap! Dragon!
Take care you don't take too much
Be not greedy in your clutch
Snip! Snap! Dragon!

With his blue and devil's tongue
Many of you will be stung
Snip! Snap! Dragon! . . .

Fanny grabbed mechanically at the flaming raisins. She wanted to cry now, long and hard. Everything had gone wrong. For some reason, her father's words and the picture of Jessie Smith running would not go out of her mind.

With his blue and devil's tongue
Many of you will be stung! . . .

Over and over it went, round in her head, with the picture of horrible Jessie Smith running home with a stone in her hand.

Now her mother was turning up the gas and a tray of hot chocolate was being brought in. Then Fanny saw her guests off, smiling, nodding, her head aching horribly, the silly rhyme and the picture of Jessie Smith beating in her mind to the banging of her headache. At last she was kissing her mother and father, and thanking them for letting her have the lovely party.

Fanny had never been so glad to reach her bedroom. A fire of logs and coal blazed in the little black iron fireplace with its pink tiles on the floor. She pulled together carefully the deep pink velvet curtains that she had helped to buy with the small amount of money she earned as a pupil teacher. She poured out some water from the big blue jug into the matching basin, and bathed her face and aching head. Then she climbed into the bed, heavy with sheets, blankets and eiderdown, and warmed by two stoneware hot-water bottles.

But she could not sleep. The party had been nothing without John. The silly rhyme and picture of Jessie kept appearing in her mind.

At eleven o'clock she sat up. There was a knock at the front door. She could hear it was nosy old Mrs Bagshaw from next door. What a cheek the old thing had to knock on her parents' door at this time on a cold winter's night. She heard the old woman's voice very clearly as it floated up the stairs and in through the bedroom door.

'I had to come and tell you, Mr Gibbs. I could see you were still up and I know you both go to bed together because I never see your parlour light on when your bedroom one is lit, so I knew I would not be waking Mrs Gibbs. I've just heard some terrible news. It's made me feel very sick, Mrs Gibbs. Somebody's murdered old Mr Dobson, by the grave of his wife in the churchyard. He's been hit over the head they say . . . ' Her voice trailed off. There was the sound of glasses and the brandy bottle being opened again. Then the parlour door shut.

Fanny lay staring at the ceiling, now glowing red from the reflected light of the coals. She had no doubt over what had happened. She did not even begin to think about the alternatives. Jessie had got John to go up the tower and throw a stone at Throttlepenny to frighten him. Fanny could see this afternoon just how much Jessie hated the old man. But the stone had killed him. Jessie was saving John from trouble.

Fanny was no fool. She knew what the trouble would be. If John had thrown a stone at the old man and killed him, John would hang. She began to shiver . . . But what if she said it was Jessie Smith? There was a slight chance they would just send Jessie Smith to prison. They could hang her, of course, but being a girl . . . Fanny was tormented for a whole hour, seeing John's handsome body hanging dead. She would never see him again. She tossed and turned and wept. Her head ached. She trembled. Her mouth was dry.

Soon after midnight, Fanny Gibbs tiptoed out of the house, fully dressed. She had decided it was her duty as a pupil teacher to tell P.C. Gratton that she had seen Jessie Smith running from the east gate of the churchyard with something big and heavy in her hand, like a stone. But because she saw herself as John's sweetheart, it was not her duty to say she had seen John drop something from the tower.

41

It was half-past twelve on the cold and frosty morning of the 7th of January 1885 when Fanny knocked at the door of the police station. She was let in quickly, and the street was left to the hissing gas behind the blue lamp, and the high winter moon.

CHAPTER
[9]

Jessie had arrived at the little courtyard in which the cottages were where she lived. She was happy, and breathless after carrying the stone. She had saved John. Her cheeks glowed red and her eyes sparkled like the moonlight on the icicles that hung from the eaves. Smut was waiting for her on the wall and he was pleased to get up for her. She put her face close to his and was rewarded with a cat kiss, cold, icy and wet, from Smut's fine black velvet nose. Jessie stroked him. The cat had been sitting on the wall for some time, watching the comings and goings in the yard, seeing if any of them could be used to his own advantage. Now Jessie was here he might get some food. He got off the wall. There was a flat square of snow where he had sat. Jessie put the stone tongue where he had been. She shuddered suddenly. The stone was covered in a cold slime, like a winter snail. The heat of her hand had melted the deep frost in the core of the devil's tongue. She would leave it there and tomorrow she would drop it in the river. Then nobody would know that John had dropped the stone.

She went straight upstairs to her tiny attic. An evening like tonight's had needed savouring a little longer in the privacy of her room. She wanted to make the jewels of today into a necklace to place in her mind, to thread all the gems together. John giving her the sweet in the shop, John waiting in the street under the gas lamp with snow in his hair, John with his arms round her on the sledge, John telling Fanny he had better things to do than go to her party . . . She lay on her mattress, her hands behind her head, arranging the events in her mind. A slab of blue and silver moonlight lit the attic and condensation on the little

43

window had frozen into a bunch of frost flowers. Above that, Jessie could see the ink-black tracery of a tree. She was completely happy.

She was awash with happiness. She swam in it, and reached out for her treasures like a queen in her palace. She groped for the blue glass beads she had bought from the Wakes Fair in July. She held them to the moonlight and smiled. She felt for the new gold sovereign she had found down a floorboard in the shop while sweeping. It was new and smooth, the gold pure and rich. She sighed. All these lovely things—and she had John too. She looked at the necklace of enamel butterflies she had bought with saved halfpennies from her wages. She fingered the cold hard brilliantly-painted butterflies dreamily. Then she took out a threepenny ring from the market with a blue stone in it. She pretended that John had given it to her. She pushed the Punishment Book aside tonight. She was so happy that she had no thoughts of revenge.

Then she left her little treasures to smile at her big treasures, as she called them. The moon, the sycamore tree above the rooftops with just a few silver sycamore keys left on his fingers. Then down the ladder she climbed, happier than she had ever been in her whole life.

Her father was dozing by the small fire. He gave her his special smile. He loved Jessie. His boys he was not as interested in, as their names, Tom, Dick and Harry, suggested. But his Jessie . . . She was worth waking up for. Her mam was asleep, exhausted, a pan of precious milk seething and hissing itself away on the fire. Jessie rescued it and fed little Tom. She sang to the baby and he gurgled at her happiness.

That done, she made a pot of strong black tea, a cheap variety she bought from the late Throttlepenny's sweepings up when he sorted out his fine teas. She made toast next, sticking the bread on the end of a long black iron fork she had bought for the family from her wages. Jessie liked to look after people, as she had looked after John tonight. She chatted happily all the time she made the toast, holding the bread steadily in front of the small fire.

'Fanny Gibbs is having a right posh "do" tonight, mam.

You should have seen what she bought for it from the shop today.' She described to her mother and father the treasures Fanny had bought. Her mother smiled at her daughter sadly. She had tasted dates, crystallised fruit, sugar plums, sugared pineapple, in her days as a maid in a big house. She knew Jessie never would. The old man never gave Jessie a treat.

'All them treasures in that shop,' said Jessie's mother, 'and he never gives thee owt. Still, we don't expect it love. It's known all round the town that Ezekiel Dobson'd throttle a penny if he thought he'd get three halfpennies from it.'

Jessie laughed and then kissed them all goodnight. She lit herself a bit of candle to finish off this happy day. She brushed her hair in her attic, her hair shimmering grey and brown, like the mice she had set free in the shop earlier. Then she fingered her treasures, held her beads to the moon, and pushed the Punishment Book even further away.

Smut arrived, proud and silvered in the moonlight on the roof, and she let him in. Then they curled up together and slept.

AT TWO o'clock the next morning, one hour after Fanny Gibbs had knocked at the door of the police station, Jessie was awakened by a loud knocking on her own back door. She curled her toes in ecstasy. She could see by the slab of moonlight that it was still only half-way through the night, and hours and hours away from getting-up time. She thought perhaps the knock was snow falling from the slates, or Mr Williams, who got drunk every night then went round the little yard, collecting washing and delivering it . . . She stroked Smut's soft warm fur and was rewarded with a short fugue of soft rumbling purring. She was warm, so warm, full of sleep and love and happiness. She drifted into deep warm sleep again.

She was awakend by her dad calling her name, over and over again.

'Jess! Jess! Jess! Come here, I want thee.' She could hear

voices, troubled and angry voices. Was one of her brothers ill? Or her mam? Or even Aunty Lily?

'Jess! Jess! Get dressed, lass, and come down. I want thee now!' Her dad's voice had altered.

There seemed to be a crowd in the kitchen by the dead fire. It was cold. There were the two Lambton bobbies, the young one and the older P.C. Gratton. The young policeman had a lantern that cast a cold hard light on everything, including her father. She was used to seeing him by golden fire and candlelight.

P.C. Gratton spoke first, his face as white and furrowed as the moon outside, as he held the lantern to her face. In his hand he held the devil's tongue that she had left on the wall. Jessie's knees turned to water and her mouth went dry. They had found out about John, they—

'Did you put this on the wall of your yard?' She must not mention John. He must be kept out of it. She must say as little as possible. But the lantern was hurting her sleepy eyes and she said 'yes' in a tiny cold voice.

'And did you bring it from the churchyard of All Saints Church?' They were still not mentioning John, so she nodded again. There was a silence. The two policemen looked at each other and then at Jessie's father. Obviously they had been talking before Jessie came down. Jessie's dad was looking at her in a strange way. Then P.C. Gratton climbed the ladder to her little palace, while the young policeman stood by her, lighting a second cruel-beamed lantern. The young policeman had been in the shop sometimes for half a pound of broken biscuits. He was tall and dark and had a moustache. Jessie had rather fancied him, because he had joked with her about breaking biscuits just for him. He had told her he liked ginger biscuits . . . But he wasn't smiling now. He had found the stone in the yard. He had taken out a pocket magnifying lens and shown P.C. Gratton the trace of blood and a hair of Throttlepenny's, trapped in the slime on the stone . . .

There were bumps and crashes in the attic. Tom and Harry awoke and began to cry. Jessie's mother, who had been crouching in a corner like a frightened animal, began to sob into her apron. Her father said not a word but looked at Jessie all the time. The two little children upstairs began to scream, and Jessie made as if to move towards the ladder. But the young policeman held her arm and it was not a friendly grasp. Jessie could feel herself going colder and colder, weaker and weaker . . . She dared say nothing, in case they got it out of her about John.

Then P.C. Gratton stumbled and lumbered down the steps. He held out his big red hand under Jessie's nose. In it was a crushed bunch of snowdrops, the gleaming sovereign, and the stolen cash book she had made into a Punishment Book.

'Did you take these?'

Again Jessie nodded. She was cold and bewildered. Why were they bothering her in the middle of the night? Was she going to be taken to prison? She began to weep.

'Is this your apron?'

'Yes,' whispered Jessie. There was a smudge of faint blood where she had hugged the stone to her. The stone had grazed Throttlepenny's scalp slightly. The two policemen looked at each other. Then the young one slipped some ice-cold handcuffs over her wrists. Before she could scream or struggle, the terrible words were spoken.

'You'd best come with us, Jessie Smith. We think you have murdered Ezekiel Dobson, in the churchyard. I must tell thee that anything you say I shall write down and it might be used against you. You must come with us—'

Jessie seemed to be caught in a cold vicious blizzard of her own screams and her mother's. She felt herself being pulled one way and another. Tears streamed down her face. She was dimly aware of hurting her wrist as she struggled with the young policeman. The cold room whirled around her and she screamed and screamed. She would not go. She would not. She had not done it. She hadn't. She had not killed the old man. Whirling lantern beams spun faster and faster. She screamed and was aware of her father sitting rock still, watching her as coldly as the moon shines through a gap in the clouds in a snowstorm. Then she must have fainted.

A terrible numbness came over her, a creeping horror of

47

coldness. Her mother gave her some clothes to take, in a sacking bag she kept sticks for the fire in. Jessie was cold and shuddering. She could feel her heart beating wildly, but one tiny spark of her earlier happiness remained in this terrible coldness. They had not mentioned John. But even that spark nearly went out when she saw her father's face as she was led away. He looked like an old and dying man in the harsh lantern light. Her mother had covered her face with her apron.

So Jessie was led away to spend the night in prison. Her father did not turn to see her go. His face was the same ashen colour as the ashes of the dead fire in the grate. And upon Jessie had settled the coldness of the ashes of her happiness. For in 1885 a girl of thirteen could be hanged for murder.

CHAPTER
[10]

IT WAS Wednesday morning, much later; but the sun had not risen yet on the frozen world, though the bell of All Saints, just below the gargoyle, had just struck eight o'clock. Had anybody looked up to the devil carving, they would not have seen any change. The tongue had fallen from deep inside the mouth. Only a trained stone mason on scaffolding would ever find there was a portion of the gargoyle missing. A plug of ice had sealed the mouth again.

Jessie was as cold and lifeless as the carving, as she sat on the narrow plank bed in one of the cells of Lambton Police Station. She was numb with fear and misery. She was as cold as the cell, with its door and tiny iron grille. There was an iron bowl, cold as the grim ice on the carved devil. There was some sick in the bowl, for Jessie had been sick with fear. Every now and again she was shaken with violent shivering. There was an iron tube containing a candle, cold and unimaginative as the law. The only colour to be seen was the blue winter sky through the bars, as beautiful as the blue beads back in her attic, that P.C. Gratton had trodden on last night.

The young policeman was not unkind. He brought her some breakfast.

'Now Jessie Smith. Why did you go and do a wicked thing like that?'

'I did not. I did not kill him with that stone . . . ' She would say no more. Still in her cold misery the spark shone. They had not mentioned John. The policeman shook her roughly but she would say no more. She was frightened of mentioning John. The policeman took her silence as a sign

49

of guilt. Then he said to her, 'You need not attend the Inquest on Mr Dobson, if you don't want to.' Jessie did not know what an Inquest was, so she kept quiet. The policeman thought the silence was her agreement not to go.

Fanny Gibbs set off for school that Wednesday morning after the murder, wearing a drab grey coat of her mother's. She did not feel like wearing bright colours. She found the gates of the school closed, and Mr Middlemas sending children home.

'We need the big schoolroom for the Inquest on Mr Dobson, Miss Fanny,' he told her. This was the way they addressed girl pupil teachers.

'Miss, Miss Fanny, Miss, what's an Inquest?' demanded one of the younger children.

'It's a sort of court where a doctor decides whether somebody has died naturally or whether they have been murdered,' said Fanny dully. Her head was aching again.

The remark brought forth a chorus from the children. 'Miss, Miss Fanny, Miss, will Jessie Smith be hanged by her neck or will they put her in prison for ever and ever, Miss Fanny, Miss?'

So, everybody knew, thought Fanny. She went to the empty classroom and sat by the tortoise stove. She had done all this to save John. She had done it for love. But she had not expected to feel so miserable. She began to cry softly by the giant iron stove. Mr Middlemas, the Headmaster, looked at her. He thought what a beautiful, sad tender picture it made. A young girl weeping for the wickedness of another. Fanny looked so lovely, her cornflower blue eyes brimming with tears, her shoulders shaking, her glorious blonde hair falling around her face. The Headmaster patted her softly. The poor, poor girl. She was suffering from shock, or thinking of that other wicked girl who deserved to be in prison. He helped her to her feet, and gently asked her to help him prepare the room for the Court. They cleared a space at the front and put a big table there. Then Mr Middlemas piled the stove with coke, far more than the children usually got.

Fanny continued to weep. Through her tears, she saw the room begin to fill with curious townspeople. They perched and squeezed themselves on to the benches. As though through a wall of shuddering water, she saw the Coroner, Dr Noble from the Workhouse, stride in and remove his top hat, bang a hammer, shuffle papers. She began to tremble violently at what she had done and set in motion. Then she felt sick and did not concentrate until she heard P.C. Gratton speaking.

'It was on my nightly walk through the churchyard, sir. It would be about half-past ten, sir. I saw his boots, sir, sticking out from behind a gravestone, sir.'

Fanny could have screamed. She had told the facts about Jessie to save John. But nobody had seen John drop the stone. If she hadn't opened her mouth, they would not have known about Jessie. She suddenly realized she was the one who would be responsible for Jessie hanging. She hated Jessie, but this . . . to get her hanged . . . She realized she had been jealous of Jessie, whom she knew was protecting John. But now, if they hanged Jessie, John would never know that Fanny Gibbs had saved him. He would always think it was Jessie. She would never be able to tell him . . . or would she? Why, why, why had she told about Jessie? To save John, yes . . . and to spoil things for them. Now she had spoiled everything. John would remember Jessie for ever. Fanny began to cry loudly. There were looks of sympathy from around the room.

She heard Dr Jones. 'I found his skull shattered as though he had been hit by a heavy object . . .' Would she ever be able to tell John that *she* had saved him from hanging, not just Jessie? But he would hate her for ever for telling about Jessie.

Now Mr Middlemas had his arm round her. 'Just tell Dr Noble that you saw Jessie Smith running away with a stone, my dear. That's all.' Fanny wept shuddering tears. 'It's your duty. They have found blood on the stone . . .' So, there was no going back. No unsaying. She could not stop the terrible events. She told the Court and knew that John would hate her for ever.

Dr Noble adjourned the Court to allow Dr Jones to give

51

the body a thorough post-mortem. Jessie would remain in prison. The whole town buzzed with excitement. Everybody knew Jessie Smith had done it. Fanny could not believe she could feel so miserable and went sobbing to bed. Everyone felt sorry for her. She wished she had never been born. She knew John would hate her for ever now: she had no tiny candleflame of joy left, as Jessie had.

CHAPTER
[11]

JESSIE, COLD, sick, alone and condemned, had the tiny glow left that she had saved John. He would save her. He would find a way out. So would her dad. Her mam, too. A tiny flame of love and hope still burned in her cold body.

Jessie's mother had begun to talk with the shock, like an alarm going off. And just as an alarm going off does nothing in itself, neither did Mrs Smith. She talked and talked and talked and talked as she saw to the younger children. 'Our Jessie'll need to look good for when they get her to court. Eat that crust our Dick and don't play with food. I'll find a good dress for her to appear in. Get out of that coal bucket our Tom, you look like a little sweep. Leave that cat alone, Harry. You know there's only Jess can do anything with him. Stop giving him that water. It's out of washing bucket.' There was chaos. The chimney smoked, the milk boiled over, the babies screamed. Jessie had been right to put her loving but helpless mother third on her list of hopes.

Her father always appeared second in her thoughts to John. He sat in the chaotic kitchen, his face white and ashen like moonlight on frosted stone. Now and again he would twist his cap round. His Jessie . . . taken away like that. He was cold with misery. He sat and did nothing. Neither parent went to the Inquest. They could not face the stares, the nods. Then suddenly, at eleven o'clock, Jessie's dad left the chair he had sat on since three that morning. He would go and see Dr Ball, the Archdeacon of Lambton. He helped the poor. He strode up to the Vicarage, staring straight ahead, ignoring the stares.

Dr Ball would be back in a few moments. He had been to the Inquest. Mr Smith was shown into Dr Ball's study, where an enormous crackling and hissing fire sent nearly all its heat up the chimney. Mr Smith thought he had never felt so little heat from so great a blaze. Neither had he expected to get so little help from such an important person as Dr Ball, D.D. (Oxon.), Canon of the Chapter of Lichfield Cathedral . . .

'Ah, Smith, my man. I have this minute returned from the Inquest. It has been adjourned. But it would seem the evidence against your daughter is strong. She may very well hang for her actions, Mr Smith. Yes indeed. But if she repents and prays to God before her execution, she may at last find everlasting peace in the bosom and arms of our Lord Jesus Christ . . .' Mrs Ball, hovering in the hall, overheard and thought what a pretty and comforting speech it was.

Jessie's father stood up. There was a light in his eyes that was not just firelight. He was no longer twisting his cap. ''er's a good girl,' he said, and walked out.

Jessie's mother was waiting outside in the road, dumb hope in her eyes. 'His Reverence says our Jessie must pray,' said Mr Smith shortly.

Sadly the family returned home, and Mr Smith set off for his work as a casual labourer. By being late he may have lost a day's work.

Jessie's main hope, John, was in the hayloft at Blackdon Castle's stables, sneaking a rest. He had spent the morning grooming horses and mucking out the fine carriage horses. Now he was snug in the best quality soft hay, happy and warm. He had a stalk between his teeth and he lay back with a half smile on his face. He lay like this for some minutes, staring at the rafters, but seeing something in his mind's eye that pleased him a great deal. After ten minutes he came down from the hay loft, swaggering a little, hands in pockets, whistling a tune. He was very pleased with himself and life.

The Inquest was opened again at four o'clock. The sun was setting over the hill to the west of the town in a tumbled sea of blood-red clouds over the village of One Ash, where

Emma Briddon lived. The red of the sunset tinted the stone devil a hellish red, making the ice fires flicker round its sunken eyes.

Dr Jones told a hushed court that the old man had died as the result of two blows from a heavy object such as a stone. Dr Noble, the Coroner, returned a verdict of murder.

At five o'clock, Jessie was given some tea and told that she would appear before the Magistrates on Friday, charged with the murder of Ezekiel Dobson on the night of Tuesday the 6th of January 1885. Jessie heard it in silence. She was now still and frozen, like a wren in its hole on a freezing night. There was just the feeling for John left, tiny as a bird's heartbeat, throbbing in her mind. She still thought John would help her.

CHAPTER
[12]

FANNY HAD set in motion an avalanche that would swallow up Jessie.

It was the custom in North Derbyshire, in the nineteenth century, to put a dead person's body on show before the funeral. This was usually in the dead person's home, but in the case of someone well known, well liked or of some importance, the body was displayed in a local inn.

Emma Briddon had made prompt payment, after Dr Jones had finished with the body, to see that Throttlepenny was laid out in a room at the Anchor Inn, for all to see. She seemingly could not keep away and spent much of Thursday keeping a vigil with the old man's body.

The stone devil, looking out high over the town, its mouth dripping water from the faint warmth of the noonday January sun, must have noticed, if gargoyles can notice, the long queue of townspeople outside the Anchor Inn, all lining up to see the body and pay their last respects.

Throttlepenny's body lay on a table, the head bandaged. Four candles burned on the table. Lily Gosling, Jessie's aunt, had been paid a very generous sum by Emma Briddon to prepare the body and clean up after Dr Jones. Lily had got busy with her scrubbing brush on the body and arranged the twisted limbs, now cold as marble. She fitted a skull cap over the bandaged head and then arranged the thin hair over that. She carefully bound up the jaw and folded the thin arms on his chest. Then she washed the body, admiring it: when she was a girl of twelve, Throttlepenny had been a fine young man of eighteen, and misery and meanness had not totally destroyed him. She

56

wrapped him in a linen gown of white, and admired the old man's rich gold signet ring. Emma Briddon had told her he must be buried with it and a small bag of gold . . . Lily thought the old man looked like a king now . . . except that his eyes kept springing open as though he wished to tell her something. Lily closed them and, putting on a big pair of gold glasses, threaded a needle. The eyes snapped open again. She closed them again as deliberately as she would blow out a candle. Then she put a small stitch in the cold flesh to keep them shut. The old man would never open them again.

The shadow of the old woman in her huge black bonnet bobbed about the room as she moved about the body putting the finishing touches to it. The corpse, Lily had noticed, was springy and bouncy. Her mother had always told her that a springy corpse meant more deaths to follow. Thinking about that, she had a little weep for her poor niece Jessie. The old woman wept small warm salt tears as she thought of poor Jessie, so unlike the cold drops that fell from the stone devil's mouth as it looked over the town.

Once Lily had finished, Emma Briddon gave her more gold. Lily thanked her, thinking she had not known Miss Briddon was so well off. Then Emma Briddon gave the innkeeper more gold for a chair and a supply of candles so that she could sit with the body. She was much talked about in the town for this action, and much admired.

So Emma Briddon sat in the shadows with the body as people filed by. There was no fire in the room, the blinds were drawn, but she did not seem to care. Now and again, as a person moved on, candlelight fell on her expressionless face, and her nose, like a winter sundial pointer, cast a long shadow.

At ten o'clock, after a twelve-hour watch, she left and walked back to her village.

As the moon darkened, over the next few days, stories about the stone devils in the churchyard and on the long road to One Ash increased. People said they had heard them laughing. One small girl, awake on Thursday night, said she had heard a devil laugh about ten o'clock at night before the moon rose.

The Magistrates met on Friday to decide what to do with Jessie. Mr Middlemas was a Magistrate, a Justice of the Peace. On Wednesday he had written in haste to London to order a new black gown for the Court. He knew a lot of people would be there. The gown had come and now he was trying it on in the small robing room, before the Court began. The gown was of a silvery-black fine silk, surprisingly like the shimmering black starlight on the midnight ice of the gargoyle. The new gown seemed to numb Mr Middlemas's feelings. 'When I taught her,' he told a fellow magistrate, 'she was a sullen girl of low intelligence and little imagination. If I had caned her more, this would never have happened.' He admired his new gown in the mirror, in a manner not unlike that of Jessie admiring the beads in her little room in the moonlight.

The courtroom was packed. Steam from melting snow off boots mingled with tobacco from clay pipes and rose to make haloes round the hissing gas lights.

Jessie stood, frozen with horror and cold, in the high dock. Nobody guessed that a little flame of hope that John would rescue her still burned.

The first witness was Fanny Gibbs. She did not look at Jessie but told the Court in a low voice what she had seen on that night, how she had seen Jessie running in the moonlight carrying the stone. She wore the purple cloak again and a bunch of snowdrops pinned to her cloak.

'You must always wear a little bunch at this time of year, in memory of dear old Mr Dobson,' her mother had said that morning. People had been so kind to Fanny, so helpful . . . but she still carried a weight of misery within her.

'And as you stood at the north gate, looking, as you said, for some friends who had been sledging, and who might have liked to come to your party, did you see anybody else in the churchyard, Miss Gibbs?' It was Mr Middlemas talking to her.

This was the moment. All she had to say were the few words, 'Yes, I saw John Mellor on the battlements below the spire. He dropped a stone.' Just those few words. Or Jessie could have shouted them across to the Magistrates. But both girls were quiet. Even if Fanny told the truth now, John would still hate her for telling first about Jessie, then about him . . . And Jessie would never never tell about John . . .

'Miss Fanny. I ask you again. This is most important. Most important. Did you, or did you not, see anybody else?'

Fanny bent her head. Everything was on her side, as it was against Jessie. She began to cry, her long lashes darkening with tears. The whole court thought how beautiful she was. It was a shame to upset her so.

'Miss Fanny, I must ask you again.'

Fanny shook her head to ease the tears in her eyes, and the tears fell upon the snowdrops. The Magistrates took the shake of the head and the whispered word which nobody heard to mean 'No.'

'Thank you, Miss Gibbs,' said Middlemas, adjusting his gown and thinking how well he had conducted the questioning. 'You may stand down.'

P.C. Gratton gave the same evidence as he had done at the Inquest. But it was Dr Jones who had the key to the mystery. Had Middlemas not been so intent on self-admiration, he might have heard that events did not fit together quite as he thought. Dr Jones read his report.

'Upon examination of the body, I found two head wounds. There was a heavy bruise on the left temple that broke the skin, causing a minor cut and some bleeding. This blow alone would not have caused death. The second wound, on the top of the head, was seven inches long and three inches deep. The wound was curved like a crescent. The skull was severely shattered, with fragments of bone lodged in the brain itself. A massive haemorrhage of blood must have caused instantaneous death. I cannot be certain if the two wounds were inflicted at the same time. However, I must tell the Court that the time between the two wounds was not great.'

'And do you think, Doctor,' asked Middlemas smoothly, 'that the defendant, Jessie Smith, could have inflicted the blows with the stone found in her yard?'

'Certainly the first blow,' replied the Doctor. 'For the second one, she would have had to bring down the whole force of the stone with the weight of her body. It would have been easier for an adult to do it with the stone. But yes, it is possible a young girl could have inflicted the wounds I saw, if she were determined enough.'

'Thank you, Doctor,' purred Middlemas. It was all going so smoothly. And there was a reporter in the court from *The Times*, taking down his every word. But he had reckoned without Jessie.

She would not say a word or answer a single question. She was frozen in body and mind, terrified . . . and she was scared of mentioning John if she did talk. Her mouth stayed shut, a frozen thin line. All she wanted was John, Smut, her dad and mam, and little Tom. Tears trickled down her white face. The people in court thought what a hard cold face she had. That thin mean mouth, so obstinate. Just standing there as cool as a cucumber, saying nothing. Everybody was certain she had murdered the old man.

Middlemas shouted at her, 'I will have a response! You will answer my questions!' He banged the bench with his fist. He saw the reporter writing down his loss of temper. Still she would not speak. So he had to send her to Derby Gaol on remand and she would appear before him again on Monday.

Middlemas was angry. He had expected floods of tears. He had had a little speech all prepared. Now he could not use it. Instead he thanked the police constable, the Doctor and Miss Gibbs. 'Miss Gibbs is always so reliable in my school. Her register is always correct and she counts the pen nibs faultlessly.' He scowled at Jessie as he dismissed her. His new gown was slipping off. Perhaps a weekend in Derby Gaol would open her mouth, he thought.

He would certainly recommend the death penalty when the time came, after this; and the time would come. The evidence was strongly against Jessie. Against the likes of Middlemas, the little flame inside Jessie had no hope of surviving.

CHAPTER
[13]

IT WAS true that Jessie had looked for John in the courtroom, but she had not seen him.

Since the night of the murder, John had been a willing prisoner in his job as one of the stable boys at Blackdon Castle. The Castle stood two miles away from Lambton, at the end of a long snow-white drive. The old Duchess of Derbyshire lived in the Castle with an army of servants, including John.

John had gone there over a year ago and had done well. The horses liked John and John loved the horses. The old coachman, Edward, had spotted that John had a way with the fine and expensive carriage horses and he took a liking to him too. The old man was teaching John a great deal about horses and carriages. In return, part of John's duties were to look after the very old man in his cottage at the end of the long street of stables at the Castle. Old Edward rarely went out of the Castle, except to drive the Duchess on very special occasions. The rest of his time he spent talking to the horses or teaching John. During the week of the murder, Edward had been ill with a cough. He had stayed in his cottage. John had looked after him, taking food up to the old man's room from trays left in the cottage by the kitchen servants. The rest of the time he spent looking after two of Edward's special horses. Edward often gave him special jobs. But it meant he rarely saw anybody to talk to. Old Edward was deaf and hated gossip. John knew nothing about the events in Lambton.

He did think about Jessie as he saddle-soaped the fine leather seats of the best Blackdon coach. He whistled as he thought about their sledging as he polished the solid silver

61

harness of the coach horses, each bit stamped with the striking serpent of the House of Blackdon. John thought a great deal as he sat by the huge fire in the coach house grate, which kept the coaches aired and ready for the Duchess's use.

But every now and again he frowned. He thought of that falling stone from the church tower. That could have hit somebody. Somebody could have been killed. If Jessie or Throttlepenny had been underneath, anything could have happened. It made him go cold and shivery when he thought about it. If the stone had hit the old man, they would have said he had done it and then . . . John knew all about how people could be hanged for killing someone, even when they said it had been an accident. When his mother got some old newspapers, she always asked John to read the murder cases to her.

On Friday, the day that Jessie appeared before Mr Marmaduke Middlemas J.P., Edward told John that he must exercise Ebony, the fine black stallion of the late Lord Blackdon, who had been killed in a skating accident before Christmas. They were waiting to sell the highly valuable horse, but in the meantime Edward was keeping a keen eye on it. John was the only one he trusted with the fine horse out of his sight, and John was only allowed to walk Ebony, and not ride him. John was to walk the stallion five or six miles along the old lanes high above Lambton.

This was a delight to John and he talked to the horse for most of the way. They rested on the high pastures to the east of the town of Lambton, called Walton Pastures, John stroking and admiring the black soft velvet of Ebony's nose. Both horse and John then looked at the fine view. Far down below was the town in golden sunshine, and the tower and thorn-like spire of the church. Once again John went strangely cold as he thought of that dropping stone. But all was fine, he thought. Somewhere down there was Jessie, and he felt a glow of warmth as he thought of her. The thought of her made him feel warmer again. Jessie had that effect on people.

He watched a train pull out of Lambton Station far below. He narrowed his blue eyes. There seemed to be a crowd at the station, as if somebody important was getting on the train. He did not know that this was the train that was taking Jessie on remand to Derby, and that the station was full of the idle and curious waiting to see her get on the train.

Something made him feel cold again. He looked at the train. The light was reflected on it in such a way that it looked like a shadowy silvery serpent winding its way between the hills and woods. Its plume of white smoke looked like a serpent's tongue. For some strange reason he thought of the carving on the church again. He shook his head. He knew what happened when you let your imagination wander in these lonely places. The hills and town still contained many strange stories and an unexplained sense of evil. He tried to think of Jessie but the warmth would not return. Strangely out of sorts, John and Ebony returned to the lonely Castle in its miles of woodlands.

CHAPTER
[14]

THROTTLEPENNY'S FUNERAL was on the following Monday, six days after the murder, and the same day that Jessie was going to be dragged in front of Middlemas again. It was going to be an exciting day for certain of the townsfolk who enjoyed such spectacles.

It began as a beautiful early springlike day, with thrushes singing and the bulbs in the gardens beginning to pierce the cold earth. But the heavenly blue of the sky melted no hearts that morning. Everybody, except Jessie's family and few friends, thought she was going to get what she deserved.

When the great tenor bell of All Saints Church began to toll for the funeral, the bell ringing just below the stone devil, the first clouds appeared in the blue sky. Emma Briddon had paid for the bell and organ and the other expenses of the funeral. People thought she was very kind and generous. All of Throttlepenny's great wealth had gone to a younger brother who lived in Buxton, an invalid confined to his room. So people nodded in respect to Emma, a good and kind woman, they thought, to see her brother-in-law off in such fine style. Most of Lambton was there, except Jessie's family.

Fanny Gibbs was there of course. She was wearing a bunch of snowdrops pinned to her cloak. She thought hardly at all of the old man. Instead, as they stood in the churchyard, her eyes looked beseechingly into the golden mists around the Castle where John worked. Would he hate her for ever and ever . . . even when . . . she brought herself to say it . . . when Jessie was dead? Then she wept at what she had done, as they lowered the coffin of Ezekiel Dobson into the deep hole. It was all so final. Fanny was much admired for her floods of tears as the coffin finally came to rest.

The gargoyle's eye glistened with melted frost as the coffin rested deep in the hole. Emma Briddon's eye glistened too behind her black veil. How well she stood and carried herself, people said. And then, just before the first spadeful of earth was shovelled on to the coffin, Emma threw in a chinking bag of gold sovereigns.

'It was his life,' she said simply, her veil hiding the triumph in her eyes.

Fanny went home with a fearsome headache. She wanted to scream and scream the truth out over Lambton, until everybody heard it . . . but she loved John too much, even though he hated her.

Emma Briddon walked home to One Ash along the four miles of lonely road. At a bend in the hilly road, by a smoking lime kiln that breathed fumes like an entrance to hell, she sat down on a disused stone trough. She began to laugh, her head tilted back, her cold stone-featured face twisted into a fearsome shape. Her cries and ugly laughter seemed to tear at the sky, covering the struggling warmth of the sun with cloud. Lapwings circled her, those strange keening birds of deceit. Jackdaws feeding in a nearby frosted field flapped back to Lambton church tower and its gargoyles. Then Emma began to walk and flap her cloak like a mad thing. But when a cart laden with coal passed her she was the respectable mourning spinster of One Ash again. And after a cup of strong black tea in her cottage and some bread and cheese, she returned the same way to attend the Magistrates' Court in Lambton that same afternoon. She was very interested to see what would happen to Jessie Smith.

CHAPTER
[15]

ON THAT same Monday after the murder, the day of
Throttlepenny's funeral, they brought Jessie back from
Derby Gaol to appear in front of Middlemas the Magistrate
again. Jessie had never had so much time and money spent
upon her in her whole life, at school or at home. There were
two wardresses from the gaol, two policemen who travelled
with her on the train from Derby. They were given a special
compartment on the train, all to themselves. Jessie had only
been on a train twice before. And now no expense was
spared. She had suddenly become a special person.

It was a springlike day, the faint warmth of the sun
lighting up the rising sap in the trees along the railway
cuttings. But the blinds were drawn in Jessie's compartment. No gleam reached her, frozen and terrified like a
winter starved rabbit surrounded by waiting stoats.
Nobody had been to see her in Derby Gaol because they
could not afford the rail fare. It would have cost her dad
one week's wages for the return fare. But she was so frozen
she hardly missed them. It was John she wanted, it was
John she expected . . . and he had not come.

There was a crowd at Lambton Station to see her arrive.
It had all worked out well for the idle and curious. The
funeral had been in the morning and Jessie was to arrive in
the afternoon. Time to get a bite of bread and cheese then
go and watch her arrive. In the station yard a crowd had
gathered and an old man was selling roasted chestnuts. A
rising wind blew the wisps of smoke around from his
brazier, and blew the sheets of newspaper. There had been
a special Murder Edition of the *Lambton Echo* to mark
the funeral of the old man. But the curious and inquisitive

saw little of note. They saw Jessie Smith held between two stout women wardresses, and they saw her stumble as she got into the special closed black police carriage that was waiting for her. Jessie had never had a carriage awaiting her before. Only the old Duchess rode in a carriage as big as this one. The heartless crowd saw her stumble as though she were frozen with cold, they saw her wild frightened eyes look into the crowd as though searching for escape. So they thought. But she was looking for John ... perhaps he would be at the Court to rescue her.

Fanny Gibbs had returned home after the funeral with a pounding headache. She had been given the morning off school by Mr Middlemas to attend the funeral. She had returned home to lie down but found she could not settle to sleep. She could not rid herself of the idea that because she had told about Jessie and kept quiet about John, she herself had become a murderer, for Mr Middlemas had let it be known he thought Jessie should hang. With this on her mind, she had returned to school in the afternoon, her head still aching and throbbing. It was still quite a fine day and she had decided to go with the children on a nature walk that afternoon. Something inside her which she could not control had turned her steps in the nature walk towards the woods and the lane around Lambton Station. Somehow the nature walk finished up on the railway bridge that took the lane over the station, just in time to see Jessie Smith return to the train which was to take her back yet again to Derby Gaol. Large drops of rain had begun to fall, but Fanny told herself and the class that they could 'run between the raindrops'.

'Observe the blackbird eating the last of the haw berries,' said Fanny weakly to the class. 'Observe the red mountain-ash berries on the tree by the platform. Observe the ash keys and the tight buds.' She was fooling nobody, least of all herself. Her eyes were on the coach that had brought Jessie back from Lambton. The children in the class were spellbound. Soon they would see a real murderer.

It had been a short hearing down in the Magistrates'

Court. Jessie had stood in the dock, white, cold, sullen and paralysed with fear. Middlemas had not even bothered to summon the witnesses again, so sure was he that Jessie had committed the murder. He had told Fanny she would not be needed in court. It was just a formality. Jessie had stared at Mr Middlemas with a white blank face. He meant nothing to her. Now and again her eyes stared round the courtroom as she searched in vain for John. She was almost fainting with fear and cold and hunger, for she had hardly eaten since her toast on the Tuesday night. Once again she kept silent, for she was scared of mentioning John. Middlemas lost his temper again.

'Very well. Very well. Very well. Jessie Smith, you are committed to trial at the Easter Assizes at Derby for the murder of Ezekiel Dobson on Tuesday the 6th of January 1885. I shall not give you bail. You will remain in Derby Gaol until your trial.'

Then she was hustled back into the closed coach and the blinds were drawn down. Some of the farm boys who had come into Lambton for the weekly Cattle Market jeered at her coach as she was driven through the town, over the bridge and up to the station. She hardly heard their boos and catcalls, or heard the heavy drops of rain begin splashing on the roof of the coach. She did not even jump when some low branches whipped and banged on the rain-smeared glass. Everything was against her. And John had not come. He did not love her. He had deserted her.

The children had climbed on to the railway bridge and were sitting with their legs dangling over the edge. Fanny was too shattered with her inner thoughts to stop them. The class gave a little shudder of excitement when they saw the door of Jessie's carriage open and the prisoner get out. They did not see their teacher hide her face in her hands for a time before looking at her old enemy and rival Jessie Smith.

'Miss Fanny, Miss Fanny, ma'am, is that the murderer?'

'Miss Fanny, ma'am, is that 'er that did it, Miss?'

'Will she be 'anged by 'er neck, Miss, at Derby?'

'Will they tie 'er ankles, Miss Fanny, when she hangs?'

'Do you get hanged in your birthday suit, Miss?' The

chorus of laughter brought Fanny to her senses. She glared at the children, perched like sooty mischievous sparrows above the railway.

'Be quiet at once or I shall tell Mr Middlemas,' she said. 'Observe the missel thrush singing on the ash tree in the storm.' Her head ached. What had she done? She felt like being sick over the bridge, once again screaming out that it was John Mellor who had done it. She too looked round wildly for John Mellor. Hadn't he done anything? For the first time, her love for him weakened a little, and the first tiny warmth of sympathy for Jessie Smith crept in. But she could say nothing now. She would look such a fool and a liar. She might even be dismissed as a pupil teacher. Middlemas seemed to want to get Jessie hanged. 'An example,' he called it.

'Look, Miss Fanny, ma'am, she's crying.'

'Miss Fanny, ma'am, did they make her wash the blood off her hands when she were taken to prison?' asked a small girl, letting her imagination run riot.

Down below on the platform Jessie was being walked to the waiting train. She heard the clear voice of the young girl and she looked up. She saw the children perched there and she saw Fanny Gibbs standing at the end of the line. She saw her purple cloak and she saw the bunch of snowdrops pinned there.

Jessie spoke clearly and loudly for the first time in a week. 'At least, Fanny Gibbs, I didn't take my clothes off for a shilling like you did in the bushes last year for the lads.'

Fanny's class exploded into laughter. Fanny blushed red with shame and then the red became blazing hatred. She stared down at the platform. 'How dare you, Jessie Smith . . . ' she said. All sympathy was gone. 'You can see,' said Fanny to the children, 'what a wicked liar she is.' But the class would not stop laughing.

A flush of colour had crept into Jessie's face. The only spark of life left to her had been her love for John and the rivalry against Fanny. Shouting up to Fanny on the bridge had been like pouring oil on the spark. It had flared up and warmed her for a moment. Then it died down, leaving Jessie colder than before and the spark almost gone. When she was hustled into the railway carriage she began to scream and cry. She felt she was sinking into a deep cold cave down inside herself. In this freezing cold ice cave she could hear her own voice screaming and screaming. She was in deep darkness in a cold cave and John's love for her was only a tiny flickering star in the cave entrance, cold, remote and distant from her. He had not rescued her.

CHAPTER

[16]

THAT SAME Monday of the funeral and Jessie's final appearance before the cold presence of Marmaduke Middlemas J.P., the Dowager Duchess of Derbyshire, of Blackdon Castle, ordered that her coach should be ready for two-thirty so that she could take tea with the Duchess of Pemberly. She would drive through Lambton, even though it was Market Day. The old lady felt in need of company. Old Edward, the coachman, was delighted. He went out rarely these days but he delighted in driving the old lady. They flattered each other. She told him he was the finest driver in the north of England. He told her only ladies like herself knew how to appreciate good driving.

Old Edward was so pleased he allowed John on to the grand shining black coach as a footman to stand by his side. There were three footmen standing on the coach, two at the back, and one at the front by Edward. John was to be the one at the front, with the pleasure of watching the old man handle the reins of the four white carriage horses. John helped Edward and the stable men put the horses into the fine black harness and its silver trimmings. John put on the horses four black mourning plumes, for the old Duchess was in mourning for her nephew. Then John changed into the silver and black of the Blackdon livery. Black coat, white shirt, black three-cornered hat trimmed with silver lace, black tight breeches, and silk stockings of dove grey. John thought it was the finest uniform in England. He particularly liked the cut of the black trousers, the fine white cotton of the shirt, and the silver lace and buttons on the jacket. He climbed up beside Old Edward, resplendent in a black suit and a ruffle of white lace, and holding a fine whip. The coach drove slowly round to the front of the Castle, crunching on the gravel, rattling on ancient cobbles. John felt high up, elated. To drive through Lambton like this! He hoped his mother would see him. They would go round Blackdon Square and Jessie would see him from the shop! And Fanny Gibbs might be out in the playground of the school. The children always ran to see the coach pass by. John stood up proudly.

John stood straight and tall as the old Duchess came down the steps. All he had to do was look good. The other two footmen put down a little ladder to help the Duchess into the coach. John stood absolutely still. Fanny Gibbs must see him like this!

Old Edward bowed. 'Good afternoon, Your Grace.' He took off his hat and put it back. 'It's a fine day for a drive. We shall have rain later, but it will be no trouble.'

'Dear Edward, I trust you,' said the old lady, and vanished into the blankets, leather and warm luxury within.

They clattered down the long drive, a fine sight. Then along the turnpike that John had run down with such happiness on the night of the murder. But the coach soon ran into traffic. It seemed unusually heavy, farmers in carts, some pony and traps, smaller carriages. Edward frowned. He had never seen the road so busy before on Market Day. John stared straight ahead, pleased with the admiring stares of farm boys and people on foot. He had no idea, and neither had Edward, that they had all come to see Jessie.

After ten minutes of almost standing still, the Duchess tapped at the glass with a fluttering white hand, rattling the glass with her emerald rings. She could see Old Edward was having a job with the restless horses, so she spoke to John.

'What a mêlée, Mellor!' quavered the old lady. 'Kindly ask someone what the hold-up is. My coach must go through. I will not wait for carts.'

'At once, Your Grace,' said John, wondering what a mêlée was.

'You, there,' shouted John, climbing down off the carriage and using the power that working for the Duchess gave you. 'Why is the road blocked? The Duchess must get through. She must not be kept waiting.'

The man was only too willing to say. 'She'll have to wait today. This Jessie Smith's more important than 'er today!'

Seeing the look of utter astonishment on John's face, the man realized that John had not heard about Jessie Smith and was more than happy to tell the story again.

'There's this young lass up in court today for the murder of old Throttlepenny, old Ezekiel Dobson. Tha knows, the grocer.' Seeing John's dumbfounded amazement, the man went on. 'Aye. This young lass Jessie Smith is up in court for murdering the old chap. It seems she hit the old man on his head in the churchyard wi' a stone last Tuesday night and killed him on the spot. Twice she did it, folk say. When she'd done it, she picked up the stone and ran from the churchyard. But this Miss, this girl teacher, saw 'er running with the stone. So she's arrested. They'll be taking 'er back up to station and back to gaol in Derby. That's what crowd'll be watching. T'owd Duchess 'll have to wait for Jessie Smith today!'

John saw it all. The stone that had fallen from the tower had hit Throttlepenny and killed him. What was that about being hit twice? What had Jessie done? But never mind that now. He was certain that the stone had fallen and killed Throttlepenny. He was right below it. Then Jessie must have picked up the stone and run with it to save him . . . and somebody, a teacher, had seen her. He stared at the man in horror. What had happened? What had he done?

The road suddenly began to spin round and weave and twist to John's eyes. He suddenly felt hot. Then cold. He went a deep red. Then white. Then he was violently sick. Then he fainted.

Neither Old Edward nor the Duchess were pleased. A footman was not supposed to be ill.

'See to your boys, Edward,' said the Duchess icily, 'before you bring them out. Has Mellor been drinking?' John had once been drunk when he was eleven and was sent away to a reform school. The job in the Castle had been given him by the Duchess to help him.

John remembered little of the journey, which had to go on, Jessie or no Jessie. He saw little of it. He was only aware of the terrible trembling that shook his body and the sweats that overcame him. He had dropped a stone on the old man and Jessie had been arrested. Perhaps she thought John was trying to kill the old man and she had hit him with the stone again . . . but Jessie was not like that. Of one thing he was sure. Jessie could be hanged for murder. He must go and say he dropped the first stone and killed the old man. Jessie must be saved. But then he realized to his shame and horror that he dared not do it. Much as he loved Jessie, he dared not go and say it . . . and be hanged.

When they got back to the Castle and John had convinced Edward that he was ill and not drunk, he went to the kitchens of the Castle, where there was always a lot of gossip, and managed to get a copy of the *Lambton Echo*. There he read the full report. Jessie had been seen running away with the stone. There was blood on the stone. It was only a small stone. Fanny Gibbs had seen her and told the police. John could have murdered Fanny at that moment. He hated her as he had never hated anybody. Yes. That was it. The stone had fallen. It had hit Throttlepenny. Then Jessie had done something else. But what? But she wouldn't. Jessie was not a killer. And he was too much of a coward to go and say he had dropped a stone. He was the biggest coward in Derbyshire, in England, the World. He reached the stone privy behind the stables, where he was sick again with fear and guilt and self-hate.

Old Edward forgave him. The lad was ill. He helped John across the yard. The rain had turned to snow and in the white snowlight John looked ravaged and ghastly. Old Edward helped John to his bedroom, a loft next to his cottage. John staggered up the ladder and collapsed in misery upon the sack mattress stuffed with hay. He wrapped a couple of horse blankets round himself and sobbed and retched in the dark.

He couldn't save Jessie. He daren't save Jessie. His hoarse sobs and coughs scattered the mice in the old loft.

He had never cried so much before. He had never realized what a coward he was. Every time he thought of going to Lambton Police Station and saying what he had done, he imagined the blindfold being tied roughly round his eyes by the hangman at Derby Gaol. He could imagine the rough rope being fastened round his neck, cutting it a little as the hangman got it into position. Then the sudden pain and darkness for ever and ever. He could not do it, not even for Jessie. He could not. But then he heard Jessie's screams and heard her in his mind calling out to him, and he could stand it no longer. He crept down the ladder and fetched one of the shining brass stable lanterns. The boys were forbidden to take the lanterns into the lofts because of the risk of fire in the hay, but John did not care any more. He returned with the lantern to his loft. At least it stopped the worst of his imaginings.

He lay there, wretched and cold. He knew now he would never be able to own up. And in this fear and self-hate he did not think enough about the mystery of the two blows. He was too busy being ashamed of himself. He wanted to shout out like Fanny had wanted to shout out the truth. But, like Fanny, he did not realize he had not got the whole truth.

John cried and cried. Now he was crying for himself and his miserable weak feelings. A sudden gust of wind at midnight blew out the lantern flame. So too had his love for Jessie been blown out by fear. Fear cancels out everything else. As soon as the flame had gone, John saw through his red and swollen eyes the stars beyond the unglassed loft window, pulsating and shimmering with light. The sky had cleared. Outside the loft was a huge ancient ash tree. Now the tree was silvered by the light of the rising moon. He stared at it miserably. The branches with their thin covering of snow looked like bones. The whole tree was like a skeleton out there in the moonlight, white and waiting. It was a message to tell him that soon his Jessie would be dead and she too would be a lifeless skeleton, rotting in the burial ground of Derby Gaol. He, John, would do nothing to save her. He clenched his teeth and turned away from the phantom tree and bit into the haysack.

75

CHAPTER
[17]

EMMA BRIDDON walked home to One Ash after Jessie had been committed for trial at the Easter Assizes by Mr Middlemas that Monday afternoon. She had walked away silently from the courtroom, not talking to anybody, staring straight ahead. She walked along the busy market day streets, buzzing with the excitement that Jessie Smith was now to stand trial in Derby at the Assizes. She had to wait as the Duchess of Derbyshire swept by in her grand coach. People saw her raise her face to look at the Duchess's coach, but they could not see her face clearly because of the black veil over her face, like a filmy shadow of night, dotted with hideous tiny embroidered purple lilies.

Emma reached her cottage at One Ash as darkness was falling and the snow was smearing the cobbles with a transparent slush. She let herself in to her large neat double-fronted cottage. Her father had been a lead merchant and had left her well provided for. Once inside, she took off her hat and veil and lit the two candles on the high mantelshelf. Her hand trembled as she did so, nearly knocking off the shelf a large china dog. In the candlelight her eyes were as wild as Jessie's had been in court. Emma gave a little whimper. She suddenly looked at her soft black kid gloves and with a little cry tossed them into the embers of the fire. Then, whining like a frightened dog, she piled sticks and coal on to the gloves until the black-leaded fire basket was full of blazing fuel and the gloves were quite gone. She covered her face with her hands as Fanny had done on the railway bridge, and sank on to her knees as though praying in front of the crackling and snapping fire. A rich pearl ring on her finger took the firelight and looked like a drop of blood.

Emma Briddon crouched in front of the flames for most of the evening. She did not eat, but kept on piling wood and coal into the fire basket. When her long case clock struck nine o'clock, she went silently up the stairs to her bedroom and stealthily drew the thick curtains. Then she went over to the big blue jug and basin she used for washing herself. She began to wash her hands in the basin with its pattern of blue roses. She washed her hands over and over again, until the lavender scented towel on its wooden rail was sodden with the cold water from the basin and smeared with Pears' soap. Now and again she shuddered and trembled.

She finally crept into her four-poster bed and drew the curtains. But it was twelve o'clock before she slept and then she was restless and kept calling out in her sleep. So it was the whole of that winter night through. She was still in a restless sleep when the thin moon peered in at the chink in the curtains and sent a sliver of cold moonlight into the room. The moonlight found the pearl ring that she had taken off and put on a small table by her bed. By the firelight the rich pearl had looked like a drop of blood on her hand. Now, on the table in the moonlight, it looked like a cold eye staring accusingly at the restless Emma.

She awoke at seven o'clock the next morning, got up wearily and made a pot of her dead brother-in-law's fine coffee. Then she went out of her cottage and began to walk quickly down Derby Lane, a lonely and now little-used lane across the high hills of Derbyshire. It was an ancient and lonely way to Derby. She strode away, her black cloak flapping in the winter wind, the plovers rising before her. But when she had walked five miles, she suddenly stopped and leaned against an old stone mile-post with its letters faded and filled with frost. She stayed there half an hour. Then she turned back. But she did not go home. Instead she took another lane that led to Summer Hay, a lonely station on the nearby railway line that led to Ashbourne. The station served a little hamlet of three farms, two cottages and a tiny chapel, that stood by the side of the main road from Buxton to Derby.

A grey sleet had begun to drive across the lonely fields

with their endless white and grey walls and smudges of snow in the grey green fields. Emma saw that the chimney to the chapel was smoking, its plume of smoke blown in the cruel north-east wind like a threadbare feather. Mr Rhodes, the minister, kept the chapel stove lit day and night for the use of tramps on the cold and lonely road. She saw him now at the door of the chapel, patting a tramp on the back. His shabby black gown was always dusty with lime that was in the air from the passing lime carts. He was a small plump kindly man. The sight of him blessing the dirty tramp made Emma suddenly burst into wild sobs that shook her dry thin body. She turned away from a passing cart carrying lime, lest the carter see her tears. She strode towards the chapel and knocked.

The minister looked at her, shocked at her pale face and streaming eyes. 'Forgive me, Mr Rhodes,' said Emma. 'I have a smattering of lime dust in my eye. I need your help, Mr Rhodes.' He sat Emma down inside the warm dusty chapel on a plain wooden bench.

Mr Rhodes began to talk gently. In his understanding of people he had found that they often did not wish to talk of their troubles straightaway. So in his kindly way he talked to Emma about the weather, how uncertain it was, how fine yesterday morning had been, and how cold it was today. And he talked about the terrible events in nearby Lambton. 'I was there yesterday,' he said sadly. 'I would like to help, but God has not shown me how yet. She will hang, of course, that poor Jessie Smith, despite her tender age. There are not enough people at present who think the law wants changing.' He stared in at the little hot cavern of the black iron stove. He did not see Emma shudder violently.

Then Emma said a surprising thing. 'I want to help. I want to help that poor girl Jessie. It was my . . . it is my belief that my brother-in-law made a lot of people miserable. He spread misery to so many people, not least to my dear, dear sister, his wife. He spread it as you spread goodness, Mr Rhodes. He may have brought about the murder on himself . . . I don't know . . . But I want to help Jessie Smith . . . I want to pay for a lawyer for her. A good one, Mr Rhodes. I've heard that young Mr Taylor down in

Lambton is very good. But it must be done privately, Mr Rhodes. Nobody must ever know that I paid for a lawyer. It is my . . . responsibility, Mr Rhodes—to help with the misery I mean, Mr Rhodes.' Emma burst into tears again as her speech became muddled.

Mr Rhodes patted her hand gently and pretended to stir the little heap of hot cinders that had fallen out of the door of the stove. He thought what a pathetic and lost creature she looked, her face red, her eyes swollen and her nose blotched with cold. Her eyes were wide and appealing to him, like a child imploring him for help. Those eyes staring at him were trying to pass a message to him. He had never seen such tragic appeal. She obviously wanted to tell him more. He did not know of her weekly visits to Lambton.

Instead he thought it was God working through this sad old woman. In his seven years as minister at this lonely chapel, Emma Briddon had trudged to it every Sunday, twice a day in all weathers. During that time she had barely said more than 'Good morning, Mr Rhodes,' or 'Good night, Mr Rhodes,' and now here she was shaking with emotion. God did indeed move in mysterious ways, thought the minister. Who would have thought of God working through Emma Briddon? Then he was angry with himself. He had no right to think that about one of God's children. Emma was a child, he saw, lost, begging with her eyes.

They knelt down in the tiny chapel, with its whitewashed walls and benches and glowing stove. He promised he would see Mr Taylor. Her name would not be mentioned.

Then he clasped her dry hot hands in his, as a blessing and a comfort. A look of horror came over her face and she snatched them away and stared down at her hands in horror, as though she hated them. Mr Rhodes smiled sadly. He thought he had embarrassed her. He watched her go up the now snow-whitened road back to One Ash. He did not know that she washed her hands three times in horse troughs on her way back.

CHAPTER
[18]

JOHN LAY in the darkness after the wind had blown the lantern out, with his teeth digging into the haysack to stop the trembling of his jaw. But the sight of the white skeleton tree outside filled him with such horror that he lit the lantern again, hearing the stable clock strike one o'clock. It was now a week since the murder, he thought grimly, and he had done nothing. And, he knew, would dare do nothing. He tossed and turned on the sack, the blankets wrapped tightly around him as though to keep guilty thoughts out. His wild awake eyes stared up at the bare rafters of the stable loft, where black dusty cobwebs swung in the breeze, and trapped leaves from the last autumn were caught in the nets of the webs, fluttering, unable to escape. So his thoughts and plans were caught up in his own fear. He could not help Jessie. He was scared of the hangman's rope himself.

His mind went back to the events of a week ago. It seemed like a different world then. Jessie leaving the shop, the snow, the railway navvy. Sam Walton's sledge, Fanny's invitation, the head of the stone devil . . . the falling stone . . . Throttlepenny still alive in the moonlight . . . the great sailing snowclouds across the winter sky, boats in the sky, prisons in the sky . . . he fell asleep with the exhaustion of everything.

He was tormented by dreams, night terrors, and they all came together in a wild nightmare as the stable clock struck five o'clock through the frosty air. He dreamed that Jessie with her face bone white like a dead girl, Throttlepenny with a skull under his black hat, the railway navvy, Sam Walton, and Fanny Gibbs were dancing round him, all pointing at him. The dance suddenly stopped and Jessie stepped forward; pulling out from under her cloak a hangman's noose. Then she turned into the ash tree in the moonlight with its skeleton branches, and John was awake on the haysack, sweat pouring off him, staring at the tree outside where the crescent moon seemed to hang from one of the lower branches like a sickle blade.

John did not sleep again. The dance kept coming back into his mind. He climbed down from his loft at six o'clock, taking care to hide the lantern until he was out in the starlit yard, where the stable chimneys were alight with moonlight and white frost. He felt numb, tired and very ashamed of himself as he did his jobs. He cleaned out the fires in the coach houses and lit them again. Then he fetched food from the castle kitchens and cooked bacon and sausage for himself and Old Edward, ready at seven o'clock. He found he was surprisingly hungry and thirsty. Not a word was said as the man and boy ate their breakfast on the wooden table, with one candle burning, and the fire that John had just lit filling the room with friendly light. Then there was a scraping of chairs on the stone floor as John collected the pots and jug to take back to the kitchen. He felt stronger but very miserable.

A faint light was just glimmering through the glass of the stable windows when he began his next job. There were plenty of stables at the Castle and the horses were moved around while the stables were cleaned. Now John was in an empty stable. He beeswaxed the mahogany partitions between the stalls, polished the brass rails with vinegar and water, and swilled and swept with a broom the herring-bone-patterned tiles. Now and again water from his eyes would mix with the water from the pail. But he could not rescue Jessie. He dared not.

The light in the yard was growing as he crossed it at eight o'clock. Streams of blood-red cloud gashed the blue above the Castle, and he felt sick again. He went into Ebony's stable and the stallion gave him his special whickering neigh of recognition. There was nobody about. John slid back the brass pole and went into Ebony's stall. He buried his face in Ebony's neck, parting the mane to reach the fine

81

warm neck. Then he cried and cried, the tears running down Ebony's glossy coat. Ebony snorted and showed the whites of his eyes for a second, and then turned and nuzzled John's ear with the soft velvet of his nose. John stayed there until he heard Old Edward's footsteps, then he wiped his eyes on his sleeve and busied himself with a comb on the mane. But Edward had sharp eyes.

'Ebony's damp, John. He's been sweating, like as not. I'll do him this morning. You go and help the lads with the hay.'

As he crossed the cobbles, the winter sun rose over the distant moors, flashing light over the wintry park, hills and Castle. John felt the slight touch of warmth on his cheek, the faint warmth of winter sun. The butterfly touch reminded him of Jessie. Then it happened. Just as the sun had suddenly filled the world with light, so something inside John opened up his thoughts. In a flash of insight came the realization. Throttlepenny had two wounds. And the navvy? He might have been in the churchyard. He had seen him go in. John's falling stone must have hit the old man, yes. Jessie must have picked up the stone and run to save him. But the second blow. He stood thinking about what he had read in the paper. There had been two wounds. The doctor had said one was not enough to kill the old man, but the second was. John saw that the answer to the whole mystery of the murder was with the navvy. He must be found.

John was filled with warmth, just as the sun was now filling the stable yard with light and melting the frost on the roof slates. He could save Jessie if he could find the navvy. Whether the navvy had done the murder or not, John was not sure. But he could help . . . and perhaps John, when he was sure of the facts, could get him arrested. But he must find him first. In the meantime, he must not say a word about the falling stone. Find the navvy first, see what he knew, or find out what he might have done. With any of the many possibilities, John felt he had now got a way to help Jessie.

John felt the danger to himself was gone. He could do something that would not put himself in danger, for he was still very much frightened by the thought of the hangman's rope round his own neck. He fetched a pitchfork and began carrying a load of hay to the stables. All the doubts and nightmares of the night before had gone. They had withered in the morning sun, just as the thin moon lay withering in the blue of the western sky behind him. He was going to rescue Jessie! He was going to save her! All would be well. He was convinced the navvy held the secret of the second, killing blow to Throttlepenny. The more he thought about saving Jessie, the more his guilt about owning up vanished. His mind was full of plans and ideas. He began one plan at once.

He told one of the stable boys to go and tell Old Edward that his mother had been taken poorly and he had to go and see her at once. Then he ran out of the stable yard and down the back drive to the long white road to Lambton. He must begin to save Jessie at once. He was out of breath when he reached the town of Lambton that January morning. Straight away he felt hurt. Nobody but himself seemed to be sharing the misery with Jessie. Life in the town that winter's morning was going on as though Jessie had never been, and certainly as if Jessie did not matter. The only sign that the world had changed was the fact that the blinds were down over Throttlepenny's windows and the shop was shut. But apart from that, everything was the same as before the arrest of Jessie. It put John off in a strange sort of way. He suddenly saw that to rescue Jessie would not be easy. He stared round at the Market Square. A horse and cart stood outside the butcher's and the horse was busy with its nosebag. A little man wearing the dusty black gown of a Methodist minister was walking in through the door of the lawyer's office. Men were sweeping up the straw from yesterday's market. He could hear a flock of sheep coming down the road.

John hesitated. He wanted to ask if anybody had seen the navvy a week ago, but he did not want to raise anybody's curiosity about his own doings on that night. He decided that the local chemist and apothecary, Mr Thompson, would be the best person to try first. Mr Thompson was a busybody and knew a great deal about the goings and comings in the town. While he was in there, he would spend the sixpence given to him at the weekend by a visitor to the Castle who had liked the way John had cared for his horses. He would buy his mother some dandelion and chocolate powder to make herself a drink to soothe her stomach with, and a tiny sample bottle of orange and quinine wine to put her in a good mood. For later he needed her to lie and say he had to be away from work because she was ill. He entered the shop and asked the chemist for his mother's treats.

'I wonder if you can help me, Mr Thompson. I'm looking for someone who might be able to help with the mystery of the murder last week.' Then he felt his own guilt suddenly stir within him, and he blushed red to the roots of this close-cut hair. The chemist did not seem to notice. John took courage. 'You see, I'd like to talk to this big navvyman that were standing outside Mr Dobson's shop about eight o'clock last Tuesday night.'

John went on to describe the navvy in some detail. He described the brown velveteen jacket with the pearl buttons, and the moleskin waistcoat. He described the fine-quality cord breeches that were tucked into the tall leather boots with their high lacing. John had noticed and greatly admired everything about the navvyman, right down to the billycan strapped to his right leg, and his neckerchief of white snowstorm spots on royal blue silk. John would have liked very much to have had the money to dress like the navvy. He had also admired and envied the man's black hair and oiled moustache. The navvy had given John a wad of tobacco to chew as he had entered the shop. John would have liked to have had the man as a workmate, and did not really want to get him in bother. But for Jessie he would do anything . . . except tell the whole truth.

'No,' said the apothecary shortly, arranging some bottles of lavender water fussily on the counter, and staring hard at John as he shuffled some tablets of wallflower soap. John shut his mouth. He realized he had said enough. 'And in any case,' went on Mr Thompson, sealing a little bottle now with a blob of wax, 'what difference will it make? Jessie Smith did it and she'll hang for it.'

John went out of the shop hastily, blushing again. He could see the town had made up its mind. It was the same at the clockmaker's. John knew navvymen wore big silver watches, and he wondered if the man had been in the shop. But they had not seen him. It was the same at the baker's and the pastrycook's. They could not think beyond the fact that Jessie Smith was going to stand trial at Derby and be hanged.

But John was not easily put off. His own guilt made him go on. He must save Jessie or live with the guilt till he died. But there was more than that. When the sun had touched his face that morning with a soft touch of warmth, he had realized just how much he wanted to see Jessie again and feel that shy gentle warm love of hers. So John found himself in an increasingly wild mood, asking all sorts of people questions.

By the middle of the afternoon, he was on Lambton Station watching a train steam out to Derby and London. He nearly got on it. He almost threatened the newspaper boy when asking if he had seen a navvy. John thought the man might have come to see where he could get work on railway repairs or new lines being built. John was big for his age and in his eagerness he nearly knocked the newsboy over. He did not know that P.C. Gratton, the man who had arrested Jessie, was watching them, for the constable had come up to talk to the stationmaster. John told him he was looking for a navvy, and why. He had asked so many people by now that he was not blushing. The policeman was rough with John.

'Look, lad. Yo' look after thy horses at t'Castle and I'll look after the law. Keep out of it, young John. Leave it to me.' John dared say no more, and he shuffled away, red of face again. The constable had closed his mind. To him the evidence was cut and dried. He had seen the stone in the yard of Jessie Smith. Seen blood on her apron. A small detail like a stranger in the town meant nothing to him. Everybody knew, he told the stationmaster, that the lad was courting Jessie. The lad was clutching at straws, he said.

John ran back to the Castle as the last of the sunset died

in a blood-red line over the western hills. The colour of the sky upset him again, and the guilt began to gnaw at him once more. The first stars were dusted over the Castle towers when he went inside to see Old Edward in his cottage.

Old Edward stood on his rag rug in front of a bright fire of coals sent down from the Castle. He turned from John as he came in and with a trembling hand turned up the lamp to full, so that the room was filled with white gold light. Then he stood and faced John, his hand trembling on an ebony stick, a gift from the Duchess. John looked round the room with pleasure. He would have to think again about what to do. In the meantime, he stepped towards the blaze, thinking how good it was to work here and how cosy it all was. On the table, where a game pie from the kitchens sent up its appetizing smell, Old Edward's top hat, made of the finest silk, gleamed in the bright light. John moved to the fire, warmed his hands, then moved to the table to set the plates. Old Edward suddenly banged down with shaking hands a sovereign.

'Get out,' he said, then began to cough. John stared at him in horror. There was silence. John heard a mouse gnawing the woodwork, a coal fall in the fire, the distant neighing of a horse, the stable clock, the whistle of a distant train . . .

'You are a liar, Mellor. Pack your bags. Take your month's wages there, tho' it's more than you deserve. You are a liar, I say. The Duchess asked me to drive her to your mother this afternoon with wines and jellies for her. We found your mother as fit as a fiddle. You are a liar. And one day you will hang, my boy. Your type always does.'

This time John went white. His face felt frozen and he felt a muscle twitching round his lips. For the old man to say that he would hang . . . But he was being pushed and shoved roughly. One of the grooms, who had never liked him, was called for and John had to give back his glorious uniform, his lovely brass lantern. He was pushed and shoved some more. He could not say goodbye to the horses. The groom threw the hard hat that Old Edward had given him down the ladder from his loft.

'You can follow it,' he said roughly. Then the door was slammed hard and John was shut out from light and from all the wonderful hopes he had had. At that moment the little flame of Jessie's love meant very little. It was as gentle as the warmth from the winter sun. Full of bitterness and rage, John trudged back to Lambton and his mother.

The walk back to John's home was soon over and before long he was blinking in the candlelight of the cottage where his mother lived alone. His father had been dead from the time that John was a baby. His mother burst into sobs when she saw him. She had known, when the Duchess had visited her thinking she was ill and needing charity and found John had been telling lies, that he would be sacked.

'Now what'll us do, our John? It's the Workhouse for me, if tha canna find a good job. I'm past mekkin' ends meet, I tell thee. I've had enough. It were your job to support me. It were a grand job you had at t'Castle and tha's gone and chucked it away.' John hung his head in shame. That was true. It had been a good job. He would never get one like that again.

'Why, our John? What were you thinking of to go and get time off this morning?' So he told her that he was looking for a navvyman who might be able to help Jessie Smith.

Never in Mrs Mellor's battered and difficult life had she been so angry. Her face became an ugly dusky red as the blood rushed to her cheeks in rage. She went over to John as though she was about to attack him.

'That little trollop? You got yourself the sack and gave up your job to help that little bag? I've seen her, John, I've seen her in the shop pretending to kick the old man when his back was turned. She killed that old man, John. It's as clear as the nose on your face. And you've given up everything to help her . . .'

John would have liked to tell his mother that Jessie had saved him from the gallows, but he didn't dare. Instead he hated his mother for misjudging poor Jessie. 'She's all right, is Jess,' he mumbled.

His mother began to cry and laugh at the same time. 'All

right is she? All right? All right? Then go after her then, go on, then, go after her. Get out. Get out. Go after her, leave me to die in the Workhouse. Go and join her. Go on, then, get out. Copy her, the little slut. Copy her life. You'll probably get hanged like her.' She began to hit John about his face, tears streaming down her own cheeks. She had given up proper food to look after John when he was a boy, and John saw her as a poor old thing. She was in fact hardly forty years of age, but her teeth were gone and her hair grey and wispy, from struggling to bring him up. John was overcome with pity. He hated to see his mother cry like this. It embarrassed him. She had now worked herself up and she hurled her weak body against him.

'Go on. Get out. Go and join her. She'll never do for thee what I've done. She'll not give up her life for thee like I've done, the cunning little bastard—'

That was too much. John lost his temper. He raised his fists to his mother. She screamed at him and pushed him to the door. He knew what he would do and nobody could stop him now. He stormed out of the house banging the door leaving his mother with her head on the kitchen table crying her eyes out.

John was crying too, but he strode out of the town purposefully towards a farm where he used to help when he was still at school. The dog knew him and did not bark. John climbed into the hay in a big barn and curled up and went fast asleep. Now he too was in trouble, like Jessie, and doing something to help her made him feel better. He slept deeply in the warm hay until morning.

The next morning, Wednesday, John was up and out of the hay, creeping away back down to Lambton before the farmer could spot him. He felt sorry in one way for his mother, who was now broken in spirit and body. He knew she had given up a lot, including proper food, to stop them from being split up and sent to the Workhouse. Yet the feeling that he was now free to help Jessie, to repay her, made him feel better deep inside himself. He would find the navvy and he would know the truth. So John thought. He walked towards the town to buy some food, before he began his long tramp over Derbyshire to find the man. On his way down he met Fanny on her way to school. As a pupil teacher, she sometimes had to be there at seven-thirty, to receive extra lessons from Mr Middlemas.

Fanny saw him striding towards her as she hurried down the steep street. She had turned her head. It was unusual to see anybody at this time, in the half-light of the January morning. Most of the men were at work. Fanny at once blushed a deep red, staring down at her highly-polished buttoned boots that peeped out of her long grey dress and purple cloak. She was glad the neat little boots had pink pearl buttons on, and she was glad she had put on her little pink shell ear-rings too. But her breath came in gasps. She had not expected to see John so soon. The part of her that looked down at her shining boots expected him to smile at her beauty and perhaps walk on. Another part of her expected trouble, boiling hatred, from him. She knew John had a violent temper and might even hit her. Now John was nearly behind her, she could hear his breath coming in gasps. It reminded her of her own sleepless sobs when she had been awake thinking of what she had done to Jessie. She stopped and stared at her boots still. Well, she had done the right thing. She had saved John. They would have got somebody, either John or Jessie. But if only Jessie were not going to die. Then she could tell John, and he would love her for ever and ever as the years went on . . .

Fanny dared to look up. The colours of the January sunrise were reflected in his coppery hair. There were bits of hayseed stuck in it. John was one of those thirteen-year-olds who look as old as they will at seventeen. He had a faint stubble on his chin and lip. His boots were filthy, smeared with the gummy mud of the farmyard he had tiptoed across earlier. He looked like a tramp on the way to the Workhouse. Fanny was at once fascinated and disgusted. In her tidy and well-ordered life, she had never been so close to anybody so rough before. Then she heard his grating voice.

'It was you as told on Jessie Smith.' His own guilt, the fact that he was to blame too, gave his voice harsh force.

Fanny moved away a little instinctively, for she sensed the violence in it.

'You cow . . . ' He could hardly speak to her now. 'You lousy pig, Fanny goody-goody-Gibbs. You bloody little sow. You tell-taling swine . . . '

Fanny's blue eyes filled with tears. The force of his hatred was a hundred times worse than she had expected. It was too much. She had done it to save him. She looked at her boots again. If only she dared tell him what she had seen. But she dare not. In his present mood she felt he would go and give himself up to the police, and then she would never see him again. And yet, just as half of her was disgusted with his looks while half of her liked them, it was the same with her feelings about what he had done. He should give himself up . . . but she would never tell him to, never! Never!

'You stinking cow . . . ' whispered John again.

'Thank you for calling me a farmyard, John Mellor,' said Fanny sweetly. 'I expect it's because you look like one yourself this morning.' She stared at him. He thought her tears were of hurt pride. They stared at each other. John was filled with hatred for her, made worse by the fact that he too, deep down, knew he should go and own up. Fanny stormed off, her boots tap-tapping down the frosty cobbles. She was all mixed up too. She hated him, and yet she wanted to comb the hay out of his hair and cook him some bacon.

But it was the hard feelings that won in Fanny. She had, after all, been able to tell the police about Jessie, knowing full well the terrible things that might happen. It was the harder feelings that won the day again. During that Wednesday at school, Fanny used the cane for the very first time and caned two boys hard. She also wrote, in her firm clear hand, in the big Punishment Book in the school. Sorting out the other children's petty naughtiness seemed to help her live with her own guilt.

Later that night, Fanny's mother told her that John Mellor had been dismissed from Blackdon Castle for not attending to his work and she must never speak to him again.

John bought a loaf and cheese in the town, just as the
navvyman had, over a week before on the night of the
murder. Then he climbed the old lane to the east of the
town towards Chesterfield. He could feel the faint warmth
of the sun on his face. He would find the navvy and at the
same time earn some good money himself as a labourer. He
was full of hope and his burden of guilt was eased. He
whistled as he walked, in between eating his bread and
cheese. A robin followed him, hopping from twig to twig,
darting for falling crumbs. Its brilliant red breast against
the blue sky and frosted twigs seemed to mean good luck.
He remembered Jessie telling him that she had a tame
robin that came every morning. Perhaps this was the same
one.

CHAPTER
[19]

BUT JESSIE is in Derby now, and all her past joys with robins and animals are forgotten. For Jessie has no past and no future.

They've half dragged her from the railway coach, over the grey platform, and they've pushed her into a waiting black carriage. This is quickly driven away from the station, away from the little crowd that watches in the rain and sleet which is glossing the cobbles in front of the station. The lamplighter is lighting the lamps in Derby but there is no light in Jessie now: just a little half-forgotten spark of hope that one day John will come.

The carriage rocks horribly over the cobbles and a loose window squeaks and whines above the clopping of the hooves. Jessie is sometimes almost thrown from her seat as the carriage turns a corner, but the people in the dark space with her do nothing to steady her. They do not even show any pity when the carriage stops and Jessie is pulled out, under the cruel glare of a large gas lamp above a door into a big building that she has not seen before. They are taking her to a part of the gaol where special criminals are kept. And they think Jessie is very special now so they are keeping a very close eye on her, saving her for a very special day soon after Easter.

They've dragged her to a long low wooden bench in a passage, but they are not letting go even though they are making her sit down. Nobody cares that she is cold and hungry, and they are not going to allow her to talk. Special people like her are not allowed to talk. They've nothing to say anyway.

Other women on the long long bench that seems to

stretch into hell are looking forward to stare at Jessie. They know she is very special. They know who she is. They seem pleased to see her, for they nod and whisper and nudge and rustle like dead leaves with a frosty wind blowing through them. But the woman with Jessie frowns and the rustling stops. And it is cold, so cold . . .

Now a thin bent woman like a witch has got hold of Jessie and is leading her away down the gaslit passage, which begins to rustle again. Then Jessie is pulled into a tiny room by the witch woman who begins to claw at her dress, the special dress that mam sent for her to go to Derby Gaol in. They've got it off now, for another woman has swum up from the shadowy corners of the room. It's like being in a deep and frozen cave under the water, and nobody cares. They haven't wiped away the tears, they've smacked them away, and the dress is tossed into a basket and never seen again. Now they're pulling at her vest, the vest that Jessie is stitched into every Michaelmas Day, the vest that stays on till Good Friday when they all take their vests off and have a bath in front of the fire, and a fish supper. Mam never lets her take her vest off in winter. Never. They can't have it. But they can. They smack her again, harder. And again. The vest comes off and Jessie curls up like a frightened kitten, but they force her straight again, these women of the deep dark cold grey cave. Now she has none of her clothes on at all.

They put hands over her mouth to stop her screams, which don't go far in this special place, this cold grey timeless bubble where special people are brought. They want to take her to a special room and wash away all of her past life, ready for the new. They've got her now in a special room where there's a big cast-iron tub. It's as big as her mam's kitchen, and underneath it burn the blue flames of hell coming from a gas pipe. The thin bent woman must be a witch because she's pulling Jessie towards this huge cauldron, where they throw you in to change you, to get you ready for the time ahead—what bit there is left. It must be a witch's brew because there's a thick scum on top of the water in the giant tub, and they are struggling to get Jessie in it. She won't go in, for she feels that once she has been in

93

there she will never get out the same, and John will never recognize her. But the women push her in, making a hole in the greenish brown scum, clotted with dirt, soap and filth, for Jessie Smith is special and will appear at the Easter Assizes in Derby, this year of our Lord, 1885.

'Wash yourself, girl,' they say. They say it again. 'Wash yourself, girl,' as though it is some sort of magic. Perhaps it is, for even the sleet and snow are clawing at a high window to try and get in to see this special prisoner.

They do not leave her in the broth too long. Perhaps she would change too much and stop being special. They pull her out, and they have some special prison clothes ready for the prisoner who will surely hang for murder at Easter. There's a rough woollen vest, prickly and smelling of other prisoners' bodies, but she is forced into it. The witch-like woman twists her arm a little as it goes through an armhole, but it does not matter, for tears can be so easily smacked away here. Then a prickly hard pair of woollen drawers are forced up her legs that are still wet from the cauldron bath. Then they bury her head in a mud-coloured petticoat that smells worse than mud. They pull and shake it into place and they pull and shake Jessie too, because she is slow and will keep on crying, and asking for her mother and brothers and a cat, and somebody called John whom they are not in the least bit interested in. There's a big sack of shoes to choose from, and it does not seem to matter if they do not fit, for she won't be wearing them for long, will she? The finishing touch is a grey prison dress, that is rough wool too, for this deep grey cave is very cold and Jessie is shivering.

'Come this way,' says the thin woman with a witch-like chin like a hard winter's crescent moon. There's a doctor waiting for her because she's special now. Doctors looked at Jessie when she had a rash and her mother found threepence for them to do so. Once she swallowed a pin in school and Middlemas took her to the doctor's because he needed the pin, but she's never had such a thorough examination from a doctor as she is getting now. Her heart is good. The doctor does not discover the little spark of love in Jessie's heart. Things like that are not noticed here. Her

94

lungs are good. Her legs are free from rickets. She will be quite fit to go to the executioner when the time comes. She can't see all the letters on the chart on the wall, and the steel nib of the doctor writes down that she can't see. But it does not really matter. It's not worth giving her glasses for the short time she will be here.

Now Jessie's getting obstinate and that will not do. They've given her soap, a towel, and a blanket that is stained from someone's diarrhoea, and she will not hold the blanket for Jessie hates filth of any kind. Even smacks will not get her to hold it, so it is carried for her into the Remand Cell, a special room for her, with tiny barred windows where snow frames one silver planet.

Jessie has arrived and they are all looking after her, ready for her special day.

Jessie did not sleep that night, the first night in her cell, the same night that John tossed and turned in the little loft above the stables at the Castle. She was cold and she would not have the blanket on her or even near her. She did not like being watched through the door by the wardress, Mrs Mont. Mrs Mont was the woman with the curved chin like a moon, whom Jessie had thought was like a witch. Jessie hated her, and the woman was with her all night through, when all she wanted was her mother and father, her baby brothers, and John. As the grim eye of Mrs Mont watched through the door flap, the first clear thought Jessie had had since leaving Lambton formed itself. Where was John? But she had no doubt that he would come.

Jessie was cold and ill by the time Tuesday morning came, but she was glad to see Mrs Mont replaced by Mrs Sugg, who was round and fat and smiled at Jessie twice, enough to make Jessie try and swallow some of the grey porridge she had brought her. She showed Jessie how to use her fingers, for Jessie was not allowed a spoon in case she tried to kill her herself. The law was anxious to do the job properly, after she had been to the Assize Court. Mrs Sugg showed her how to polish the porridge bowl before she sent it back, how to polish the brass bowl in the cell for washing,

95

where to empty her chamber pot, and how to arrange the copy of the Bible and Prayer Book on a little shelf in the cell.

So the first Tuesday passed for Jessie. There was another meal at three. At night yet another wardress came, a Miss Stenton, with a pointed wolf-like face and no chin. Her cold eyes watched Jessie spend her second night in the cell.

Jessie never did learn the proper names of her wardresses. She couldn't be bothered. Yet her imagination, the imagination that she had used in those far-off days in the shop, came to her rescue. She called Mrs Mont 'Mrs Moon' to match her curved back, curved chin and cold face. Round fat smiling Mrs Sugg she called 'Mrs Sun'. Wolflike, thin, distant Miss Stenton she called 'Mrs Star'.

So the days began to pass. Thursday. Friday. Saturday. Sunday. On that first Sunday night the tiny candleflame of love for John flickered and went out. He had not come. She was trapped for ever and ever. She began to kick and scream in her lonely terror and Miss Stenton and Mrs Mont tied her down, for she was violent, and they put a gag in her mouth to stop the terrible screams. Now Jessie felt truly alone in the cell, alone with the cold and the stars and the cold moon. John had deserted her. He had left her alone to die for him.

But the next day, Monday, almost a fortnight after the murder, Jessie had a visitor. It was not John, but it was somebody who had every intention of helping her, if only to make a little more money for himself.

Mr Taylor had walked up to Lambton Station for the ten o'clock train to Derby. He had walked slowly up the hill to the station, twirling his walking cane as he went, enjoying the song of a lark and a good cigar. He was in no hurry to get to Derby. Emma Briddon had given him a very generous sum of money to act for Jessie. There was no hurry. Her trial was twelve weeks away yet. Plenty of time to see her, pleny of time to catch a train. He strolled into the station and bought a firstclass ticket, then went to warm himself by the blazing coal fire in the First-Class Waiting Room.

The train came steaming in slowly and Mr Taylor waited

on the platform, puffing at his cigar, until a porter found him a compartment to himself and showed him into it. Mr Taylor settled in and checked the time with his gold hunter pocket watch that shone and glittered in the sunlight shining into the compartment. The sun glittered on the brass door handles and lamp of the Midland Railway first-class compartment. Mr Taylor seemed at one with it, with his gold hair slightly oiled and curling, lying against the red velvet head-rest. He sighed and gave the porter a shilling for bringing him a footwarmer of shining copper filled with hot water. He took out a pair of gold-rimmed wire glasses and began to read a collection of newscuttings about the case. He was looking forward to it very much. He was delighted Miss Briddon had paid him so very well. He had every intention of getting Jessie Smith out of prison. He was determined she would not hang. If he got her off, then his name would appear all over England and he could set himself up as a lawyer wherever he chose, and not just in Lambton. He stroked his silk top hat, smiling a little. All girls found him charming and always fell in love with him. He expected Jessie Smith would, and he expected the truth from her within half an hour.

He took a horse cab from the station at Derby, enjoying the sight and sounds of his county town. He entered the prison smoothly, almost gliding in the door and smiling warmly at Miss Stenton outside Jessie's cell. Miss Stenton was impressed, and liked his teeth, which he showed when he smiled.

Then he was in the cell. He sat on the plank bed with Jessie and introduced himself.

'Hello, Jessie, my dear. I'm Mr Taylor. You might have seen me about in Lambton.' (A dazzling smile was directed on Jessie.) 'I have been sent to help you and save you from prison. I am a lawyer and I will help you in every way.' Then he took Jessie's cold white hand and held it tight in his, a little trick that worked wonders with the widows of Lambton but seemed to have no effect on Jessie whatsoever. Her hand lay cold and limp in his big warm one, as though she had been in a deep cold cave underground. So he tried another trick.

'Would you leave us, please?' he said to the wardress, Miss Stenton. He turned on another toothy smile. She thought him charming.

'Well, sir, it isn't regular ... ' A silver half crown gleamed in the wintry cell, which would be carefully charged to Emma Briddon. The wardress went. 'And could you bring a good wax candle please ... it is so cold and dark in here.' After the warmth and glitter of the Midland Railway, Mr Taylor felt the cold. After the candle was lit, he started on Jessie, her hand still in his.

'Now Jessie, were you quite quite alone in the church-yard with Mr Dobson? Was there anybody else there?'

Jessie turned her tormented eyes upon him. Who had sent him? What did he know? Was he trying to get John into bother too? She said nothing and they sat in the grim cell, the flame of the candle stretching and reaching up in the cold airs. He asked her the question again. And a third time. He had too much at stake to give up.

'I was on my own,' said Jessie softly.

'But some children had been sledging, had they not? Surely there were other children there?'

She said nothing. She looked at the floor which she had scrubbed seven times with cold dirty water since last week. He reached in his pocket and took out a bag of striped humbugs, that glittered like glass wasps in the white paper and candlelight. That will work, thought Mr Taylor. It did not.

'Jessie, did anybody give you the stone to hide? ... Are you shielding anybody? ... Did any grown-up person make you do it?' He was no fool. A slight tremor passed through Jessie's body at the question 'are you shielding anybody', but her body was too cold and unhappy to show it much, and besides, he was beginning to lose his temper. Miss Stenton, peering through the door flap, was convinced that the silence was a sign of guilt.

Mr Taylor began to dislike Jessie. The pale face, the large eyes so full of fear and life, yet telling him nothing. The thin mouth closed in an obstinate line, the hair hanging in unwashed greasy strands. She was stopping him from making something of the case.

'Jessie, for one more time. Do you want to tell me anything?' Silence. The jingle of Miss Stenton's keys outside the door, a jackdaw chacking on the roof, a scream, the whistle of a distant train . . . She must be guilty. Well, he was not finished yet. He'd come again. In the meantime, he patted her as he would an obstinate horse and put the blanket round her. At once she came to life and threw it on the floor.

'Don't you want your blanket?'

'No, it's got muck on it.' He called for Miss Stenton and got it changed. He could see she was grateful for that. So, he'd be back.

'Have you any messages, Jessie, to take back to Lambton with me?' Again he saw he had done the right thing. She sent her love, she said, to her mam and dad and to her brothers, Tom, Dick and Harry.

'Anybody else?' asked Mr Taylor innocently.

'Just give my love to John,' said Jessie softly.

'Who?' asked Mr Taylor sharply. She told him. He was disappointed at the answer. He had hoped for a clue. 'Oh yes,' he said, picking up his top hat and empty notebook. 'I've heard of that fellow-me-lad. He's got the sack from Blackdon Castle and now he's gone missing.' He got ready to go. He had missed the only clue. He said goodbye to her, telling her he would be back perhaps next week.

THAT MONDAY night, after Mr Taylor's visit, John did come to Jessie. He came to see her in her cell. Her imagination put him there. When Mr Taylor had told her he had run away she was sure it was to rescue her, and the little flame that had gone out the night before was lit again, and she wanted him to be with her. Her imagination made him stand there in the small square of moonlight, while she lay on the bed with the blanket pulled round her neck. He stood there with his cap in his hand, the moonlight lighting up his hair to a tarnished silver. She thanked him for trying to rescue her, and told him all that they would do together when they got out. They would teach the robin to take crumbs from John's hand, and she would buy a blue collar from the market for Smut, and some fish heads, because he liked those. In September they would go and get nuts from the woods for their mothers, and when it was hot they would take little Tom to paddle in the river . . . So it went on. Mrs Sugg looking through the flap would marvel at the girl's beautiful eyes as she lay awake in the moonlight, and wonder if she was praying . . . But the days went on and John only came in her dreams.

CHAPTER
[20]

MR TAYLOR, John and her family were not the only ones who wanted to get Jessie out of Derby Gaol. So did Fanny Gibbs. She now knew she could never live with herself after what she had done. She could not sleep at night. Worry about it was spoiling her looks. What was the use of saving John's life, even if he would not speak to her, if it made her too ugly to look at? Fanny had several plans of action.

But it now looked certain that Jessie Smith would hang unless something was done very quickly. It was February. Time passes quickly when death is waiting for somebody. The Easter Assizes would be held in April and there was a chance that Jessie would be executed by the end of April. Unless somebody did something.

Now the February rains were here. They poured down on Derby Gaol, making rivers of soot-smeared water gurgle in the new cast-iron gutters on the gaol roof. The sparrows who lived in the gaol roof cowered from the stabbing cold rods of rain, while under the slates a cold and numb Jessie scrubbed the floor of her prison cell, watched by the witch-like Mrs Mont. Then Mrs Mont watched Jessie empty her chamber pot down a grille that was chuckling with rain water. Jessie's thin weak and terrified body retched into the drain, and her sick mixed with the rainwaters from the roof; Jessie had not yet got used to the prison stink.

While Jessie was carrying out her prison tasks, the rain poured down on Emma Briddon as she splashed down the long wet road to Lambton, her hands, white and wrinkled, emerging from the ends of her black coat. Her hands were deadened, wrinkled and sore with so much washing and she liked to feel the cleansing drops of the early spring rain on them. Emma was going to buy some more Pears' soap from Mr Thompson the apothecary. She used a large amount of soap these days.

The rain splashed and poured down on John Mellor as he pushed a barrow of heavy wet clay from a railway cutting that was being rebuilt at Belper on the Midland Railway, only a few miles from Jessie . . . But John thought there was plenty of time left. That's what he kept telling himself. Plenty of time to do something, find the navvyman. But there was not much time. Already, in London, the Crown was preparing its case against Jessie, and the snowdrops on the heap of earth that was Throttlepenny's grave were now withered with the passage of the days. But it was Fanny more than anyone who saw how time passed.

It rained heavily as she walked home from school. It rattled and drummed on the stretched green silk of her umbrella, and dripped on her cold hands that clasped the ivory handle. Her hands were as cold as Jessie's, as cold as Emma's . . . but her face burned red under the watery green light of the umbrella for she kept hearing a terrible rhyme in her head. It was a horrible skipping rhyme that the schoolgirls had made up, and the boys chanted it too. Mr Middlemas had banned it and said he would cane anybody who dared to say it. But Fanny heard the rhyme chanted in the distance as she walked home. It floated out of alleyways as she splashed up the Derby Road, and was heard from behind high yard walls, and it beat in her head, which always seemed to be hurting these days. The rhyme had a horrid rhythm:

> Throttlepenny's cold and dead
> Jessie Smith has cracked his head
> Teacher went and told the tale
> Now Jessie'll hang at Derby Gaol!

Shaking her head and her umbrella, Fanny went into the post office. She would put a stop to the rhyme and she would put a stop to her own misery. She had had enough. She bought three red penny stamps in the post office and walked out with a determined air. Then she walked home with a quicker step. She knew what she would do.

She took her coat off in the hall of her house, calling to her mother who was in the sitting room. 'I won't come in, mother. I have lots to do before tea. I'm going upstairs.'

She was going to put a stop to it now for once and for all. There was a bright fire burning in the bedroom and she held her cold hands to it for a moment. She admired her fine nails in a moment of pleasure. And where was John now? . . . Would she ever see him again? . . . Sighing, she stood up and turned out the bright gas light above her desk. She wanted to do what she had to do by the light of a candle. It seemed more fitting somehow. She lit a wax candle in a blue china candlestick and put it on her desk. She picked up her best pen, the one carved out of ivory with a gold-plated steel nib. She opened up her ink-well, a travelling one of brown leather with a silver spring lid. Her father had given it to her when she had been told at school that she was clever enough to become a pupil teacher. The lid was shining silver and had the letters FLG inscribed on it, Frances Louisa Gibbs. Well, she was going to write to the Queen. She was going to confess. She selected a big sheet of her very best blue writing paper.

---

4 Victoria Terrace,
North Lane,
Lambton,
Derbyshire.

Wednesday 4th of February, 1885.

Madam,
In January I reported to a Magistrate's Court that I saw Jessie Smith running away with a stone. I now wish to withdraw my statement.

No! That was no good. She screwed it up and tossed it into the fire. All that was right was the 'Madam' bit. She had looked that up in Middlemas's big book on letter writing. She stirred the ashes of the letter angrily with the small brass bedroom poker. Why, why, why had she told? Jessie Smith had spoiled everything. She would have got John off her in the end. Well, she might get him yet. She would try again. She got to her feet and went to the big oval mahogany mirror on the wall. She put on her new round gold wire glasses and decided she looked quite good in them. Her mother had taken her to Buxton to see an optician because she was getting so many headaches and her eyes were so red and swollen some mornings. She sat at her desk again. The glasses gave her confidence.

Madam,
As an act of mercy and Christian forgiveness, I would like to
withdraw my statement about seeing Jessie Smith running away
with a stone in her hand. I did see her running away but I do not
feel she should hang.

No! The first bit was good but the rest wasn't. Oh well, if at first you don't succeed, try, try and try again. Her mother's voice called her for tea. She would write it at school tomorrow. She would put all the sums she could think of on the board and the children could do them, and she would write the letter at the teacher's desk.

She arrived early at school next day and filled the board with long multiplication of money, ready for writing the letter. But after the bell went, the Headmaster, Mr Middlemas, said he wished to teach the whole school. He was going to tell them all about something that would take their minds off that worthless girl Jessie Smith. He was tired of hearing about the little coward. Fanny said nothing. She was the only one in the room that knew Jessie was not a coward, and she wanted to scream and scream as she saw the whole school put together, the partitions in the classrooms pulled back, and Middlemas unroll a huge map. She rubbed her forehead. Her head ached again.

Middlemas showed the children a map of Africa and he pointed to a place called KHARTOUM. He told them that a very brave man called General Gordon had just been killed there by the natives. General Gordon, he told the school (who were still much more interested in Jessie), had defended the town with just a few men. Nobody came to his rescue. The soldiers who were to rescue him never came. He fought bravely on. But at the last he had to give in, abandon all hope, and die.

A loud sob came from Miss Fanny. It was the story of Jessie all over again. The children nudged and giggled. The lesson was becoming more interesting than they had at first thought. Middlemas glared round at his school and picked up his cane.

'The Queen is very cross and sorry that nobody helped General Gordon. Very cross that nobody did anything.' (Another loud sob from Miss Fanny.) 'Her Majesty is so cross she has sent a telegram to Mr Gladstone, the Prime Minister, and one of my London friends has written to tell me what was in the telegram. I am going to read the Queen's telegram to you. We should all help brave people.' There was another sob from Miss Fanny. Middlemas beamed at her. What a kind softhearted girl she was. He cleared his throat for the Queen's words.

'The news from Khartoum are frightful and to think all this might have been prevented and many precious lives saved by earlier action is too fearful to consider.'

Fanny burst into loud sobs, much to everybody's pleasure. Middlemas thought it gave added meaning to his lesson. The children thought it good for a laugh. But the Queen's words were shuddering through Fanny's brain as she wept on the high-backed teacher's chair . . . 'and to think all this might have been prevented . . . precious lives saved by earlier action . . .'

'Dear Miss Fanny, you are right to weep for General Gordon, a brave, brave man!' boomed Middlemas. 'Now children, compare General Gordon to the worthless Jessie Smith. Would she have died to save anybody else? Of course she wouldn't! Would she have kept fighting on till the end to do her duty? Of course she wouldn't! What I have said to you all this morning is a lesson for us all.'

The classroom screens were rolled back. Miss Fanny was helped by Miss White to the teachers' room and smelling salts were waved under her nose. Those terrible words beat in her brain, 'and to think all this might have been prevented . . . ' She would never dare write to the Queen now, for the old lady sounded as if she was in a right old rage. Fanny could hear the terrible words hurled at her if she said something now. She staggered back to her class, who were fascinated by her red and swollen eyes. Fanny wound the gold wire of her glasses round her ears and began the lesson.

'Miss, Miss Gibbs, Miss Fanny mam,' said a small boy. 'Did the natives hit that General Gordon wi' a stone like Jessie Smith did, Miss Fanny mam?' Middlemas's plan had not worked.

So Fanny walked back home again through the churchyard. Still the words of the Queen's telegram to Mr Gladstone drummed in her mind, and she looked up to the church tower where she had seen John, almost a month ago, drop the stone. If only she hadn't said anything. If only . . . She should have gone to John and told him that she had seen him drop the stone. Then the burden of guilt would have been on him. She would have been able to help him, give him advice, and he would have loved her for it, and nobody need have known, and Jessie would have hidden the stone, and she would never have said a word.

She put her hand on her aching forehead. One of the gargoyles near to where John had stood seemed to be blocked up. It was spraying rainwater from its mouth. Perhaps it was damaged. It was spluttering water at her, high up on the tower, as though it was laughing at her.

CHAPTER
[21]

OF COURSE John wanted to save Jessie from the gallows, from choking to death on the end of the hangman's noose. Of course he did. He told the little voice so that kept nagging him to do more, that little voice we all have, that can be so critical of our actions. Of course John wanted to help Jessie. He told his little voice so a hundred times a day. It would just take a bit of time sorting it out, that was all.

John had found work easily as a labourer with one of the gangs of navvies who were always about in Derbyshire in the 1880s, improving the new railway system, building extra tracks, reinforcing tunnels, cuttings, bridges and drains. John was quickly taken on by the foreman. He was young. You could pay him a low wage yet get almost a man's work from him.

Now it was early March. John had been working with the same gang of navvies and gangers on improvements on the Midland Railway between Belper and Derby for eight weeks now. He had free lodging in the navvies' huts, more meat than he had ever eaten in his whole life, and plenty of beer too. There was nothing like a few big white pots of beer just before bedtime on the wooden bunks to stop the little nagging voice inside him, or stop the horrible dreams about Jessie swinging white and pale on the end of a long long rope that he was holding, a rope that seemed to get shorter each time he dreamed the dream.

Now it was March. He knew Easter and the Assizes must be only weeks away, and Jessie's death would follow soon after. The little voice of conscience nagged and nagged him deep inside, as he wheeled barrowful after barrowful of earth and stones on the railway track.

'You've asked all the men on the camp about the big navvy, and nobody has seen him or heard of him. So it's about time you moved on. Time's getting short,' nagged John's little voice. Well, he might come for work, mightn't he? There was plenty of work here and the navvyman might come one day soon, and he wanted a bit of money to send home to his mother in Lambton anyway. 'If he's not come now, he won't come at all,' said the voice. Well, the men talked a lot round the fires at night, he might hear something soon, pick up a clue, so he may as well stay here, mightn't he? 'You should go and find work at the other end of the county,' said the little voice. Well, he might soon, but there was plenty of time left, wasn't there? And if the navvyman turned up here, he was only a few miles away from Derby Gaol, and he could go and get her out quickly. That was why he was staying here, wasn't it? And he wanted to buy his mother a clock, she'd always wanted one, hadn't she? It would make it up to her for his leaving home like that. One picture that kept coming into John's mind was that of his mother putting her hand over her eyes and squinting at the church clock to see what time it was. 'Go now,' said the voice sternly. 'You know it's nearly too late already. You've got to go now' But what if he ran out of money? He'd be no good to Jessie dead in a ditch, would he? He'd once seen a tramp dead in a ditch from hunger, hadn't he? He'd go in a few days. 'Now,' said the voice. 'You must go now.' But he wanted to save some money in case Jessie needed a lawyer, didn't he? He was just getting to know all the men and talk to them about their workmates in other camps, wasn't he? 'If you don't go now, it will be too late. You are a coward. You're going to let her die to save your own skin. That's it, isn't it? Go on. Admit it. You're—'

John shook his head to rid it of the little voice. It was dinner time and he walked off for a moment by himself. The sun was warm on his face. Suddenly he wanted Jessie again by his side. He looked around him. He felt in his pocket and pulled out five gold sovereigns. He'd plenty of money for weeks to come and to give his mother some. A hazel tree above him on the embankment waved its golden catkins at him and a blackbird sang. He could feel all around him the gentle gold warmth after a night of frost. A gentle warmth that reminded him of Jessie.

'If you don't go now, you may never find him. If you don't, you'll have to own up and you'll hang. If you find him, it may save you.' John groaned aloud and climbed up to the golden hazel tree on the top of the embankment. The sun was warmer here on his face. He thought of Jessie and her warmth and laughter. Without looking back to the camp of men, he squared his shoulders and went. He crossed a ploughed field where the plovers called, and reached the main road.

There was a milestone on the road that said DERBY 2 MILES CHESTERFIELD 23 MILES. He sat on it and realized he was almost sobbing with fear and emotion. He was angry with the little voice inside him. All right, he'd show himself. He'd walk away from Derby and Jessie. He'd take the Chesterfield road. He'd show it. Serve everybody right if he never got another job. This was the second one he'd walked out of. He might not be so lucky next time.

He walked along the white road that led northwards, and the sun shone on his back and made him sweat. The little voice was quiet for quite a time until he came to Chesterfield in the late afternoon sunshine. He stared at the crooked spire, almost in tears again. The spire was crooked like his life. He thought he might stay the night in Chesterfield Workhouse. That at once set the little voice of conscience off again. 'What good will that do? You must keep on walking until you find a railway camp and stop there. Go on. The trouble is you're yaller. Yes, yaller. A great yaller coward—'

'Bloody shut up!' shouted John aloud, much to the amazement of the Market Square of Chesterfield, which saw a tall dirty youth, unshaven and wild, swearing to himself. John was so angry he walked on at a great speed out of the town, on and on and on, half in tears, until he could walk no more and sat on a gate. Now look what he'd done, he told the voice. Soon it would be night and he didn't know where he was. He ate some bread and cheese that he'd bought at the navvy shop that morning and at once felt better. It shut the voice up too. He looked round. Fields and fields . . . but there! Over there. There was a low brick tower. It was puffing out breaths of white smoke to the east wind like a contented dragon. It was the smoke stack of a tunnel. Where there were tunnels, there was usually work. He relaxed and ate his food and drank at a trough. Standing up again, he saw a cart approaching, laden with red bricks and iron pipes.

The carter nodded his head at John, and John climbed on. 'Looking for work, lad? There's work to be had at north end of Bradway tunnel, two miles along. That's where I'm going. They're getting a gang of navvies up there.' The little voice inside John said it had told him so.

It was true. There was work to be had at the north end of the tunnel, a long tunnel that took the new Sheffield to London line under the hills to Chesterfield. There had been a big landslide on the cutting where the tunnel began. The carter pointed out some huts in a field, close by the little Dore and Totley Station, and John went over and asked for work. He got it. So it was back to the old life and he had done nothing, he told the little voice and himself. But he was wrong. He had done a great deal.

Work began at four the next morning. John was heavy-eyed and miserable after a restless night in the fleas and straw of a hut. He joined a gang who were to dig out earth from the landslide that had covered the down line for a quarter of a mile before the tunnel entrance. He set off to go with them when a voice called out.

'Lend us that young lad, Bert. I want some lad to walk the tunnel with me before the Leeds express comes through.' The foreman nodded at John. He went. He didn't feel like wheeling barrowfuls of muck. And the little voice had been nagging again. 'You didn't ask anybody last night when you were eating thy grub, did you? Another day wasted . . . '

'Right, lad. What us does is this,' the man was saying. 'Thee walks wi' a lantern in front. I walks behind thee wi' this ickling pole to knock icicles from roof of tunnel. Dunna worry if one clouts thee o'er they head!'

It was as cold as the grave in the smoke-filled tunnel and they did just what the man had said. John walked in front flashing the lantern and the man knocked down huge sooty icicles. Although the weather had turned springlike, there were still hard frosts at night and the icicles were a danger to the trains. John was overcome with deep gloom. It was like a hellish grave. It was like walking under the churchyard. It was like a cold prison. The tunnel was over a mile long. When they were nearly through, it was getting light and John saw the tiny circular star of daylight at the end of the tunnel with such joy he nearly cried out. Then he suddenly realized. This deep dark long underground tunnel with its hellish icicles must be what Jessie's life was like now. She was in a cold grave like this. And the only light at the end of the tunnel for her was him. This time he did not need the voice to urge him on.

When they were out in the cold March morning sun, he began to talk to the ganger. 'I'm looking for this navvy,' said John, blurting out his description, though not saying why he was looking for him.

'I know him,' said the ganger, comfortably puffing his pipe as they sat a moment in the sunlight at the tunnel entrance. 'I know him. It's Handsome Jack th'art seeking.' John stared. Not at the name but at the fact that his quest was over. Finished. Now he knew the navvy's name he would find him. All the navvies had nicknames. Long Harry. Fiery Fred. Uncle Joe. Dirty Dick. Terror. Guzzle. Taffy. Lincoln Harry. You never knew their real names. Now I shall know the truth, thought John. 'Aye. I saw Handsome Jack only yesterday. Girt big bugger, fancies 'is chances, always dresses like a toff. Watch 'is fists tho'. He'd flatten thee. Aye. I saw him yesterday. Showed me his bag o' money. Never seen so many gold sovs together. I dunna know where he can have got all them from. He telled me he were going to booze all day up at Totley, and all night. Then he were going to spend next night at Workhouse at Ecclesall an' get cleaned up like. Th'all find him toneet at t'Workhouse.'

111

'Where's this Workhouse?' John was trembling. Soon he would find out the truth and see whether he would have to own up himself . . . if he ever could.

The ganger told him. Then, for the third time, that afternoon John walked out of his work and made his way to one of the Sheffield Workhouses at Nether Edge.

A little voice inside John nagged him all the way down the valley road that led to the Workhouse. What was worrying John now was not the little voice that urged him on to ask for the navvyman. No. It was the fact that if Handsome Jack had been mixed up in the murder of Throttlepenny, he was not going to admit it to John. He would not suddenly say, 'Right lad. You dropped the first stone but that did not harm him much. It were me that hit him a second time, that killed him.' It was the uncertainty that was so frightening. Perhaps the navvy had not done it, perhaps he had seen something else . . . but why had he not come forward? Did he have a conscience? All these questions John tormented himself with; because he knew that the only other way out for Jessie was for he himself to own up, and he just could not see himself doing that, whatever the little voice inside him said.

He followed the ganger's directions and walked slowly up the hill to the Workhouse. Night was coming on, frosty and clear. The Workhouse was in a posh part of Sheffield called Nether Edge and John could see, over towards the town in the north east, a million gas lamps twinkling, cut and gashed here and there with the blood red lights of forges and foundries a long way off. Behind him a full moon rose, silent, solemn and cold. The tramps and vagrants were waiting by a side entrance in a long queue. Just twelve men in front was Handsome Jack, the man he had been hunting for nearly two months. There he was, head and shoulders above the other ragged men, strangely smart in his cap, his velveteen jacket—that looked a new one—his neckerchief of silk. John felt the feeling of admiration again. He would like to look like that. He did not dare approach him and jump the queue. The men were silent with cold and hunger and despair, and John wisely waited his time.

John had never been in a Workhouse before, although he had heard many tales about them as horrible places designed to make people want to work instead of going into them. The file of men moved slowly forward and John at last came to a stout oak door that was standing open. It reminded him of a door into a church or a castle. There was a small porch and in it sat a man at a desk. The man next to him was putting a silver half crown into his mouth. 'If you've any money on you lad, hide it. They'll not take thee otherwise.' When nobody was looking, John slid the gold sovereigns he had into his mouth too.

The man at the desk did not even look up when it came to John's turn. A gas flare danced and wobbled in the cold air behind the desk.

'What is your name?'

John spoke with difficulty. 'John Mellor, sir.'

'In which parish were you born?'

'Lambton, sir, in Derbyshire.'

'Your age?'

'Sixteen, sir.' A lie. But he did not want to be sent home to his mother just when he had found the navvy. But nobody noticed or cared.

'When did you last work?'

'Belper, sir.' Another lie. His mother said liars always ended up getting themselves hanged. Well, it might come to that. He shivered suddenly.

'Where will you go tomorrow?'

'To Lambton sir, to see my mother and then to look for work.'

He was moved on. A man in a sacking apron gave him a hunk of bread out of a large basket. Another man handed him a thin slice of wet-looking cheese that smelled strongly. John saw the men in front wrapping up the food in their handkerchiefs and he did the same. Then they went into another room and John saw to his horror that the men were being asked to strip naked. He did the same and blushed. Even at the navvies' camp at Belper he had never had to do this. His clothes were taken from him and he was given a pink card ticket with 'No. 68' printed on it. He put this between his teeth, again copying the other tramps. His clothes and handkerchief were taken away.

Then he followed a long queue of naked men to a big room with a large iron bath in it, much bigger than the one Jessie had suffered in. It was possibly even filthier too. The water steamed in the cold air but it was gravy coloured with filth from sixty-seven men who had already been made to wash in it. Little clusters of hair floated on it and lice and fleas darted and jumped on the surface, like escaped punctuation marks. John felt sick. He could see Handsome Jack walking through the water, waist deep in the sludge, swearing and laughing. Well, he'd have to follow him. That's why he was here. John bravely followed. Just as Jessie had thought, two months ago when she was plunged into her filthy bath, that she was doing it to save John, so John thought he was doing it for Jessie. He also knew he was doing it for himself. The next few hours were going to be the most important in his life. He was given a square of towel that was almost like a sack but it was clean and he was able to rub away most of the slime and filth of the bath. Then he was handed a nightshirt of prickly wool, a haybag to sleep on, and a clean blanket. He was moved on again and given a tin bowl of soup with some meat in it but mostly potato. He had to drink this standing up, then he was shoved forward again. The men were told that they were to go to a place called 'the shelter', a sort of barn. The Workhouse was full. There was no room in the cells and tramps' dormitories. The hard night frosts had brought a lot of the tramps indoors.

There was a cheer from the men around him, now all clad in rough ankle-length nightshirts so that they looked like a group of mad monks. 'You can have a bit of fun, a laugh and a talk in there,' he heard a man behind him say. John shivered again. 'That means you can get to talk to Handsome Jack,' the little voice said.

John found himself in a barn packed with men and youths. The best places, free from draughts, were around the walls, and they were all long taken. John found himself a place near the middle of the barn. He put his haysack down by a big iron pail of water and a pile of tin mugs for the thirsty. John sat down on the sack and looked cautiously around. Handsome Jack was over by the wall. He seemed a popular friend and some tramps had made a space for him. He had his back to John and was talking and laughing in a low voice to some other men.

'I can't do anything yet, can I?' John asked the little nagging voice. He heard the clink of money and guessed they were playing cards for money. He wondered how they had got the cards through the bath.

All went well for quite a time. John accepted a smoke from a young tramp near to him and asked how they had got tobacco and cards through the bath. 'Carries it in your armpits, like,' said the tramp. 'They only seem to want to clean the lower half!'

By ten o'clock John was dozing. By eleven o'clock he was woken up by the increased noise. Some of the men had secreted in little bottles of spirits and these were being passed round to friends. By twelve o'clock some of the men were singing. The Workhouse authorities were very strict inside the actual Workhouse. But on nights like this when they had to put men in here they were short staffed and nobody took any notice of what happened. They even left the gas flares on the wall alight.

At one o'clock a long tall thin man with rusty steel-framed glasses began to dance and sing. They were vile and shocking songs that fascinated John but made him feel ashamed for listening to them. The man stood in a square of moonlight and the other men egged him on. There was no way John could get to Handsome Jack.

For the second time in twenty-four hours John realized what Hell was. It was not a place of flames and devils with pitchforks like Dr Ball had told them at school. No. It was a place where people were behaving as badly as people can. It was being trapped in a cave of cold misery, with only one tiny distant cold star of hope that the navvy might help. There was a big chance that star might vanish. John did not know it but his hell was almost identical to Jessie's. Both of their stars of hope were fading.

Then the thin man began to edge towards Handsome Jack and point and laugh. The two men were either old

115

friends or enemies. John sat up to get a better look and the moon moved with his body, as though trying to get a better view through the window. The thin man then began a very insulting song.

> As Handsome Jack was passing by
> He stepped on a powder keg
> It blew him high into the sky
> And blew off his middle leg!
> Oh! Dig boys! Sing boys! Dig!
> There's gold at the end of the line!
>
> Now Jack he missed his middle leg
> As any navvyman should
> So Jack fetched hammer, saw and nails
> And made one out of wood . . .

It was one of the cruder navvy songs and John had heard it many times before. He turned away in half-bored and tired disgust. Then there was a roar like that of an angry bull. It was Handsome Jack. He did not like the use of his name in the song. He was standing up and shaking his fist at the thin man. The thin man continued with the song and Handsome Jack began to step over bodies and sacks to get him. The thin man skipped and hopped to where John was and Jack caught him there. The thin man was drunk and clutched at Jack's nightshirt, tearing the thin wool at the neck showing Jack's hairy chest. John was reminded of fighting animals and tried to back away, but there were so many men now sitting up to watch the fun. Jack shook the thin man back and forth for minutes, snarling at him like a wild dog. Then he raised a huge fist, his eyes savage with temper. The fist cracked across the thin man's jaw and knocked out his teeth, which flew through the air like white moonlit bees.

John hardly heard the uproar. Those fists. He was convinced at that moment that here was the real murderer of Throttlepenny. Those giant fists. The temper. John could imagine the man inflicting the horrible head wounds on Throttlepenny. Throttlepenny would only have had to say the wrong word to this man. Here was the murderer. But how to get him? How to bring him to justice? He's the real murderer, not me, thought John and even the little voice did not argue for a time.

'Gi' us water,' John heard Jack say. He realized he was talking to him. John broke the tranquil moon reflection in the pail as he lowered a tin mug into the water then handed it to the giant. He dared to look up at the big man. John saw the angry eyes and bloodied fists and trembled. Jack threw the tin mug back into the moonfilled pail and grinned a little as it splashed John. Here was the murderer. Here was somebody who would stop at nothing.

The fight had calmed the men down. They slept and snored. John tossed and turned. 'You either get him arrested or get him to own up. Then you and Jessie will be free. Or you'll have to own up to save Jessie,' said the little voice. But I daren't do either, thought John as he buried his face in the sack and slept with sheer exhaustion.

At six o'clock they were awakened and they collected their clothes from the bath-house. Then from six till nine the men had to work. John and Jack and another man were sent to the Crank House where they had to turn a big iron handle to grind bones to make bonemeal for farmers and gardeners. The stench in the house was foul from piles of rotting bones and tramps' half-washed bodies. The work was easy for Handsome Jack turned the wheel effortlessly. John had to keep telling his voice to shut up. For now he had found Handsome Jack he was too scared to ask him anything.

They were given fat bacon and bread and hot sweet tea at nine o'clock in a room with the other tramps. John sat himself next to Jack. There seemed nothing else to do. Jack, stuffing bacon in, suddenly spoke to John.

'I know thee.' This was it. John went hot and cold and began to shiver. 'Go on then,' said the voice. Then John did the bravest thing in his life. The nation was at that moment thinking still of General Gordon and his bravery, but John's act of bravery was never discovered. 'Now!' said the voice.

'I saw thee in Lambton on the night of Ezekiel Dobson's murder, the one they've got Jessie Smith for,' said John. He swallowed. 'I saw thee outside his shop and then I saw thee go to churchyard just before he were murdered.' John expected the giant fists to crash down on him. In a way he hoped they would. He could not cope with much more. John made himself look at the handsome face. Did a shadow pass over the tanned skin? Was there a slight twitch of the mouth muscles? Did an eyelid tremble?

'Aye, that's right. A rum business that were. I could tell thee a strange tale, lad, when the time's right, but there's few that would believe me.' He looked at John jauntily but his eyes were watchful. Threatening? Suspicious? John could not tell. He dared say no more yet. Even the little voice realized that. All the time he was eating John could feel the power of the man by his side, even though Jack did not say another word to him. But he had not forgotten him. When the meal was over the man said, 'Looking for work, lad?' He did not wait for John to reply. 'There's still plenty on the railways. I'm going Lambton way. Walk with us.' It was a command. John could sense the danger in that command. He was in an unknown land now and plans could no longer be made. He would have to live it minute by minute.

They walked in silence for an hour, past the rich villas and woods to the south of Sheffield, past the Dore and Totley Station where he had been yesterday. Not a word was said. All John's admiration for the man had gone. It had been replaced by fear, for himself and the future. Twenty minutes' walk from the station brought them to the high moors. Still nothing was said. John felt caught up in a web of mystery and fear. Above them was an invisible net of larksong in the March sky. It seemed to trouble the navvy. Three times he picked up a gritstone coping stone from the roadside wall and threw it high into the sky with a roar of anguish or anger—John could not decide which. John could feel the man's power and strength—and his watchfulness. He could feel a power pulling him towards the giant. A carter taking coals in the opposite direction thought they were father and son. But still the navvyman said nothing, there was just the wind in last year's heather and the larks. The navvyman seemed to walk closer. Then the little voice inside John said an amazing thing. 'Watch him. He's going to kill you. You know too much.'

118

From that moment on John walked in fear. He was relieved when they walked down the long hill into Baslow and the silence was broken by hens and blackbird song in cottage gardens. But the man got hold of John's arm as they were crossing the old humpbacked bridge over the Derwent. For a scaring moment John thought Jack was going to push him into the snow-fed swirling waters of the deep river. Jack took out of his fine coat pocket a leather bag. John was certain he had seen it before. But where? Where? There was so much to piece together. Jack had taken a gold half sovereign out of it and was giving it to him.

'Buy thysen some baccy an' booze, lad. Tha looks as if tha needs it. I've plenty of them.' He nodded towards the half sovereign. He winked at John. For a moment John liked and admired him again, wanted him for a workmate. Then fear took over and he trembled. The navvy nodded and they went on their way. It was as though he were pulling John by invisible threads of power that John could not resist. Jack whistled as they walked up the long winding road that led to Lambton, known for miles around as Thirteen Bends. John tried counting them. He was totally confused now. Was Jack being friendly?

Half-way along, the man sat down against a cast-iron milepost and took out a bottle of port wine and half a cheese. John stared. The man seemed to be rolling in money. John drank the rich wine and ate the good cheese and at once saw things differently. They walked on and Jack whistled to the thrushes and blackbirds in the sun. John found himself counting the bends in the road again to try and take his mind off the battle in his mind. Was Handsome Jack a friend or a murderer? They walked down the long road towards Lambton. Just before Lambton Workhouse Jack said, 'When the time's right, I'll tell you a right story about what I saw. But I want to work alongside you a bit first . . . ' And he grinned at John. It could have been a smile of murderous intent or friendship. John still was not sure. He bent down to do up his bootlace outside the great iron gates of Lambton Workhouse.

He heard a woman cry from inside, 'Jane Mellor! Jane Mellor!' He looked up puzzled, for that was his mother's name. Then he heard the sound of running feet and to his amazement he saw his mother, dressed in a long grey dress and carrying a washing basket. Somebody had seen him outside the gates and called his mother. She was in the dreaded Workhouse. She was at the iron gates now, looking through at him, thin, pale, crying, her hair a horrible grey.

'The Duke's agent turned me out, John, when I couldn't pay the rent. Said we had to be made an example of, John.' She began to cry and John felt himself going cold with horror and hot with embarrassment. 'They said you'd thrown a good job back in the Blackdon family's face and I should have brought you up better . . . ' She began to rock backwards and forwards. They had her prisoner now. By the look of it they were making her work in the laundry. They had told her this was what you deserved if you could not support yourself. 'God knows I tried to bring you up right, John.' John could only stare and weep silently himself. So they had no home now. He felt in his pocket and pulled out the five sovereigns he had earned on the railway and the half sov the navvy had given him. Here was enough rent for at least a year.

'Too late, John. I'm finished . . . I shall end my days here . . . Too late, John . . . too late. Chasing after 'er.' The thought of Jessie being responsible brought fire back into Mrs Mellor for a short time. 'Five pounds? What good is that? They've taken all my furniture, clothes. I've nothing. If you get a cottage with that, how are we going to live? All because of 'er.' She reached through the railings and knocked the gold coins into the white dust of the road. 'Look at you. You're like 'er, that Jessie Smith. You've been drinking. You look like a tramp. All because of 'er . . . if your father knew what you'd done to me because of 'er, he'd never rest in his grave.' That was too much. John bent to pick up the gold and his tears made little black marks in the dust. He heard his mother being ordered back to work.

When he felt pulled round enough to look around, Handsome Jack had gone. He had vanished off the face of the earth. Half of him was glad. The other half wanted to cry with frustration. So near and yet so far. He knew he had been in a trap of some sort, and yet . . . he mustn't give up. It was either him or Jessie . . . and he knew he could never own up . . . He must find Jack again, even though he feared the strange power the man had over him. And his mother . . . what would become of her? The minutes passed into hours as John sat by the roadside, his head in his hands.

The sun, now high in the sky for spring, began to dip to the west. The coltsfoot round John's battered boots began to close its petals. John for the moment just could not take any more.

Jessie was left to her fate.

CHAPTER
[22]

EACH DAY the sun grew stronger, climbed a little higher in the sky in its race to midsummer. Now it was April and Easter had come and gone. Every day since January a sunbeam had shone in Jessie's cell when the weather was clear. Over the weeks it had shone in a different place as the sun climbed higher in the sky. Now the beam of sun was creeping towards her plank bed with its one blanket. When it shone there, her execution day would have long passed. The sight of the sunbeam made her scream and weep. It reminded her too much of the lovely outside world, of the birds and flowers, her family and John, and walks by the river to see the ducks. One sunny day in late February she had screamed for three days and was put on bread and water for a week. In the fine weather in March they had to tie her down again. Only when the moon shone through the high bars and the greenish glass of the high grimy window did she feel better and could her imagination work. Then she could think of John.

One morning in late March, a Sunday, she had heard a shout at the back of the prison chapel and had turned round thinking it was John come to take her away. But it was not. Her food was stopped for a whole day because she had turned round. Since that day, over two weeks ago, soon after the time that John lost sight of Handsome Jack, Jessie had found it harder to make John stand in the moonlight. He seemed faded to her as though he had stopped caring, as though something had gone wrong. But she knew that could not be true.

Jessie's Judge arrived on Saturday the 11th of April, all

ready for the Easter Assizes the following week. He was called Mr Justice Gault. Jessie's prosecution arrived on the same train but not in the same compartment. English law tries to be very fair and the Judge might not discuss the case against Jessie with anybody. The man who was going to prosecute Jessie was Mr Philip Grindle-Ford Q.C. He was paid by the Crown to make the very worst of Jessie and do his best to get her hanged. He was paid to find out as many nasty things about her as he could. Emma Briddon was still paying privately for Mr Taylor to help Jessie. He wanted to get her freed and to be famous for getting her freed. He was still struggling to find out nice things about Jessie. Mr Grindle-Ford and Mr Taylor would battle it out in court, the Judge would listen. Then he would decide.

Mr Grindle-Ford thought it was an easy case. Smith would be sentenced in two days, he thought. So too did Mr Taylor but he would hardly admit it, not even to himself. He hated to be on the losing side. Over and over and over Mr Taylor had questioned Jessie. He had got nothing out of her. No reply. He had come almost to hate Jessie. He questioned her closely week after week about John Mellor. There was something there, he was certain. The girl was covering something up. Whenever he spoke of Mellor, the girl's lips went into a thin line. Her eyes would look to the wall as though she dared not trust herself even to mention his name. Mr Taylor wanted to shake her. He even wanted to smack her hard for her own good. He would like to see Mellor hanged in her place. He would feel he had done a good job if he could achieve that. Not that there seemed much chance. She remained obstinate and silent.

Mr Taylor's pride was hurt. Jessie did not even look up at him with admiration when he walked into her cell. Although she would not open her mouth to say a word about John, she would talk, just, about other things. He was sure he was going to fail. He hated failure. He had written once to Emma Briddon. 'I am wasting my time and your money,' he had written. But she had written back that he must help the girl. She would double his fees.

'Please keep on, Mr Taylor,' she wrote. 'Paying for Jessie Smith's defence is my way of thanking God that all has gone well in my life, though it has not in others' through no fault of their own.'

So Mr Justice Gault would listen to Mr Grindle-Ford and Mr Taylor and would then judge Jessie, with the help of a jury. Not Jessie's mum, who knew what a help she was when things went wrong or the babies cried all night. Not her little brother Tom who loved her soft and gentle ways and missed her bedtime stories to get the boys asleep, stories the tired Jessie would tell until they were all asleep. Not Emma Briddon who knew more than anybody about Throttlepenny's mean ways and how they could drive you to murder. None of these people would judge Jessie. Mr Justice Gault, aged sixty-four, would do the job.

Mr Justice Gault sat on the sun-warmed leather seats of the open carriage that had been waiting for him at Derby Station. He was a cold thin man, but he had never been in a cold hell like Jessie had been, in her deep cave since January, or John had been, in the Workhouse or the ice-filled tunnel. He had never had to search dark cold wintry landscapes for single distant stars of hope. He had always lived in sunshine and he drove in it now down the road from the station. All was glitter and warmth. There was a procession of the Mayor and Corporation of Derby in front of him. The April sun shimmered on the Mayor's gold chain. Then came a regiment of soldiers marching in honour of the Judge. The sun shone on their polished badges and brass buttons. The sun was shining on all of these important people with its full glory. And all Jessie got in her cold cold cell was a spear of sunshine, that pointed like an arrow to her terrible future.

The sun shone on the Judge and Mr Grindle-Ford and the soldiers when they went to Derby Parish Church next day, Sunday 12th of April. They seemed to attract the golden light. Sun streamed in through the windows as though to melt the hard brass and marble within the church, and possibly the hearts of the Judge, Mr Grindle-Ford and the soldiers. Outside, in a fresh green spring-leafed tree a blackbird sang its pleading song ... but nobody listened. They listened politely instead to the Reverend Dr Ball, Archdeacon of Lambton, who had been

124

invited to preach the Assize Sermon. He took as his text Hebrews 13, 'Remember them that are in bonds', and when they had listened to that they prayed and were ready to judge Jessie.

Jessie's mother was cold. The sun did not touch her, nor the springtime. Derby was a long way from Lambton and none of the family could afford the fare. She had tried to walk it one fine day in March but had only got as far as Matlock. Now Mr Taylor was using her. It was very important for him to get Jessie freed. So he had decided to get the mother into Jessie's cell to see if she would make her speak. He had paid the fare for Jessie's mother to come to Derby and had added it to Emma Briddon's bill. He had put Mrs Smith in a third-class compartment then settled himself into the sunshine, plush and winking brass of a first-class one. He got her out on Derby Station and the frantic woman bought Jessie sixpennyworth of fruit, pears, oranges and grapes. It was fruit Jessie had never tasted before and never would again.

When the tears were over, mostly the mother's, she said, 'Eh, Jess . . . why didst tha hit him? A blind man on a galloping horse could have found thee out when tha hid t' stone in our yard.' But Jessie never answered, much to Mr Taylor's fury. Jessie was past that. She seemed to see her mother at the end of a long cold tunnel. She was numbed with fear and depression, and bewildered that John had not yet come. Jessie and her mother clung together but Jessie's terrified eyes stared at the sunbeam on the whitewashed wall and her body was as cold as ice.

It had been an utter waste of time, Mr Taylor thought angrily as the train steamed back northwards to Lambton. His angry eyes searched the gangers on the railway tracks every time he saw men on the line. Had Mellor found work there? For some reasons Mr Taylor blamed John, and would not rest until he was sentenced to hang instead of Jessie Smith.

On Monday they got the courtoom ready for the Assizes. It

took a full day to polish the wood and clean the windows so that the sun could shine on Mr Justice Gault and Mr Grindle-Ford. The brass rails were polished too, so that Jessie would be dazzled by the hardness and sparkle of the law.

That day Mrs Mont told her that tomorrow was the day of her trial for murder. Jessie stared at the wall and two tears trickled down her cold cheeks.

That night the sun seemed unwilling to leave the sky and it took a long time to become dark. When the moon shone in, it was thin and cold and the picture Jessie made of John was ghost thin.

'John,' she whispered, 'Mrs Moon says my trial is tomorrow. You will be there, won't you, John? Only it's getting late, John . . . you will be there tomorrow, John?' But John could not answer her.

CHAPTER
[23]

JOHN HAD spent a frenzied three weeks searching for
Handsome Jack. Always searching for the big man, always
knowing that he had ruined his mother's life, always
knowing that he had cheated Jessie of her life.

He went down to Derby again. Then he walked the lark-
strung hill roads to Manchester. Then he went over to the
east as far as Huddersfield, over grim moorland roads
where the bones of winter snow still lay under dark walls.
He found no trace of Jack, so he went down to Barnsley and
the railway there, but they had never heard of Jack. Then
he trudged to Doncaster and back to Sheffield, all in two
days. But there was no sign of the navvyman. He stopped at
gangers' work on any railway line, enquired at navvies'
huts and camps. Nothing. Then he began the trek all over
again, walking the same roads, following the railway lines
that divided up Derbyshire like the life-giving veins of a
leaf. They gave life to John too, for they were his last hope
of life for Jessie. He walked the high roads, his boots ringing
on the stones, his heart hammering. 'Try the Great
Northern line Doncaster way . . . you'll have to try the
North Stafford line Ashbourne way . . . get over to Buxton
and see the working on the London and North Western . . . '
All he thought of was Jessie and railway companies.
Sometimes he walked thirty miles in a day. He had been to
the Great Central line at Chesterfield five times now.

He thought spring and hope would never come as he
traipsed the long wild roads. Dark woods by the roadsides
clawed at him and the rooks cawed endless advice to him as
he marched along. Cold winds from the east numbed him.
And always the little voice raged within. 'You've made a

right mess of everything, haven't you? A right mess. You know what you should do to save her? Go and say you dropped the stone from the church that killed him. Dr Ball would come to court and say he had seen you in church. Everybody would believe you. And you're glad that Handsome Jack's gone because he frit you. Admit it.'

The war within John began to send him almost mad. Coal carters, lime carters, drivers of cheese waggons, road menders, began to talk of the crazy boy seen on the London Road, sometimes at night, shouting and swearing at himself, his eyes wild, his clothes filthy and in rags. They had seen him in moonlight in a ditch on the Manchester Road at Rotherham, arguing with something unseen on the roadside. They had seen him waving his hands in a snowstorm on the London Road at Doncaster. He wore out five pairs of boots. He became the talk of five counties. He slept under railway arches, haystacks and by lime kilns with other tramps, who were scared by his mutterings and sudden bursts of tears. He lived on bread and cheese and beer, and once, at the Bull i' th' Thorn on the London Road out of Buxton, he had become drunk and thrown a stone at his reflection in the glass of the window. He hated himself so much. The stone had hit an old farmer in the parlour and cut his cheek. The old man said he could remember the days when a lad could be hanged for doing that.

At the Cat and Fiddle Inn on the Macclesfield Road he drank too much again and frightened a farm girl going home late. Farm girls were told to be in before dark or to go in twos. They said this young man wanted putting away. At the Malt Shovel Inn down at Shardlow they talked about how they had seen him foaming at the mouth and hitting himself as he stood by the River Trent. He looked as though he was about to throw himself in. A good thing if he had, people said. At the Moon Inn, Stoney Middleton, they said he was lying in wait to frighten little children on their way to school. The police at Derby were told. A farmer in the tiny village of Dore, near Sheffield, said he would shoot him if he caught him in his haystack again.

It was fortunate that he returned to Lambton on the day that Jessie's trial began because he was very close to being hunted down and imprisoned himself. The apothecary saw him in the Market Square, muttering and swearing aloud, and told that gentle old lady Miss Emma Briddon that he feared the boy was going mad. 'Talking to unseen people is the first sign, you know.' Miss Emma Briddon said nothing as she bought her soap and hand cream for her sore chapped hands.

John had nowhere to go. It was the day the Assizes started and he just did not know what to do next. Despite the torturing voice, he could not give himself up. He had thought at one time he could . . . but when the time came he knew he never could. He wandered aimlessly into the great woods to the east of the town, woods where in better times Jessie and himself had gone ghost hunting. Now he didn't care if he saw a ghost or not. He crept into the farmyard of his best friend Samuel Walton, who lived on a big farm at the top of the hill beyond the woods.

Sam had heard his father talking about John. 'They say since the lad's lost his job, he's gone soft in his head. Well, I never did like him. There was always something sly about him. I could never trust him when he used to come and see thee Sam. If I see him round this farm, I shall get my gun to him.' This was meant as a warning to Sam, because John and he had been best friends in the last days at school. Sam took no notice. He knew what it was like to be picked on and alone.

He saw John the next morning as he was taking the milk churns out of the yard in the horse and cart, down to the station for the milk train. He saw John in the wood near the farm, wild eyed and crashing through a glade of bluebells. Sam left the milk cart and ran over to John, telling him to hide in the wood until he returned. He left him crouching like a frightened animal behind a tree. On his return, an hour later, all the farm men and his father were at breakfast and it was easy to get John into a hay loft. He told his mother and father he had seen a fox in the wood and asked to take his bread, eggs and bacon outside, to watch. Just this once. They let him.

He gave the food to John in the loft. Sam stared at his friend, embarrassed by his dirty clothes, the dirty fluffly stubble on his chin, the way he tore at the bread and bacon and eggs.

'What's up, John?' said Sam at last.

John just shook his head, and Sam was further embarrassed to see he was crying.

'Tha can stay here and sleep,' said Sam wisely. 'Nobody comes here, it's old hay me grandfeyther left. There's only me who comes here. Toneet I'll bring thee as much food as tha can eat.' So that day John did know peace of a sort. He did not know it was the first day of Jessie's trial, that she was looking for him in the courtroom, and that horrible things were being said to her.

That night Sam brought John pies, milk, cake, and the last of the Bow Cross Farm autumn apples. John ate and ate, and at once felt better, for he had been living mostly on bread and cheese. He felt at peace for a few moments. Bow Cross Farm was a big farm that employed seven men. There were many lofts and barns and they would not be found. Neither would Sam's mother miss the food, for she fed the men who worked on the farm and cooked in large quantities. So both boys stretched out comfortably in the sunshine that filled the old westward-facing loft. Swallows looped and skimmed around them. They had arrived that very day, the first swallows of summer, and they were exploring their old nests. At their feet Tissy, the ancient farm cat who could scent trouble a mile away, purred. A cuckoo called in the green froth of new leaves in the wood below. All the warmth and light and hope suddenly reminded John of Jessie and he started to cry again. Sam was puzzled and did not know what to do. He put a hand on the filthy smelly jacket John wore, then took it away again.

Between sobs, John told Sam how he had seen the navvyman in the churchyard on the night of the murder.

'Tell the coppers then,' said Sam.

'No, it's no good, Sam. They found blood on the stone Jessie had.' Sam saw him nearly crying again and did not dare say that perhaps Jessie Smith had done the murder. And John did not tell him that he had climbed the church tower and a stone had fallen. Sam could not understand what was troubling John but he could feel the misery. When the farm kitchen was empty, Sam stood on tiptoe and stole a whole sovereign from the toby jug on the mantel-shelf. His family had got plenty, he thought. His grand-father had been a rich man. They kept finding pots of gold hidden all over. Sam could not think of anything else to do. John needed help. He would give the sovereign to him.

Next morning Sam's father climbed out of bed at four and saw Tissy the farm cat in the yard, waiting outside the privy. He watched. The cat nudged the door open. That meant there was somebody inside, for the old cat liked to rub round your legs as you sat on the lavatory seat. Soon after, Tissy came out followed by . . . a young tramp? No! That young varmint Mellor. Sam's father reached for the gun that he always kept in his bedroom and shouting angrily threw up the window. He fired at John, aiming at the cobbles at his feet.

'Get out! Go on! Clear off our land. Go on. Get out that gate or I'll put some lead in ye, so help me.' He watched John run away through the mist, the old cat following him with her tail up, as though it were all a game.

Sam's father burst into Sam's room angrily, asking if Sam had seen John. Sam lied and said he had not. But he was glad he had stolen a sov for him.

John bought some bread and some hot pork in Lambton. People were looking at him as if he had stolen the coin so when the sun came up over the eastern hills he took the road to One Ash. He looked dirtier and more dishevelled than ever. A governess, passing in a pony and trap with the children she cared for, told the children to spit after they had passed him, in case there were fever particles coming from the young tramp.

The hot sun beat down on his back. The second day of Jessie's trial was warm for April, a perfect spring day. John did not know this. He did not know where he was going, what he was doing. He just walked on, aimless and heavy with misery.

The home-cured bacon Sam had brought him last night had been very salty and when John reached One Ash he had a terrible thirst. There were no wayside troughs on the high hills near the village, so he knocked on the first cottage door he came to.

Emma Briddon came to the door. He asked her for a drink of water. He did not know that she had been in the churchyard on that fateful night. She did not know he had. All John saw was a very old woman, with a face twisted with misery and grief. She fetched him a cup of water in a cup without a handle. She watched him drink it, leaning her shaking body against the door post.

'I know what it's like to live in hell,' she suddenly said. John, if the same remark had been made to him a year ago, would have thought the old woman mad. Now he had suffered himself he just tried to smile at her. He knew eactly what she meant. Emma had started to say that she lived in hell. The village folk of One Ash were beginning to say she was going mad. John did not think so. He understood how it was possible to live in hell. But he did not want to know her problems. He thanked her for the water and handed the cup back to her outstretched, trembling hand. Then he went.

John did not know where he was going now. Neither did he care. He was finished. He could do no more. He was a coward, a failure. He walked slowly on, down the road from the village, to the little station and hamlet of Summer Hay, where Emma Briddon had walked in January to persuade the chapel minister, Mr Rhodes, to let her pay for Jessie's lawyer. But John did not know this. All he knew was that his head hurt. That his feet stung and burned with the corns on his feet. Each time he had bought a new pair of boots, he had had to buy cheaper ones. He hadn't time to wait for a cobbler to repair any of them. The hot sun made icy rivers of sweat trickle down his back. His body was worn out from the battle in his mind.

Outside the tiny Methodist chapel of Mr Rhodes he collapsed. He could go no further. He lay there in the cool dust, crying, his head throbbing, the little voice yelling at him.

A carter from one of the lime kilns saw him and carried him into the little chapel. Mr Rhodes came hurrying towards them. He was used to this sort of thing. The road from Buxton to Derby was one of the loneliest in the county. He supported John and helped him to a room at the back of the chapel, where he had set up a temperance bar for tramps, carters, railway navvies. Mr Rhodes did not call them tramps. He preferred to call them 'gentlemen of the road'. He had made the bar a few weeks ago when a navvy camp was built, three fields away. The London and North Western Railway was going to straighten out several bends on the High Peak line. He wanted a bar for the navvies that only served tea, coffee and lemonade. He believed that beer made working men into brutes.

He helped the miserable John on to a stool and gave him a big white mug of hot strong sweet tea. Then he gave him another.

The minister began to talk to John. He felt great anger that a young boy of John's age should be wandering the roads with no work and in rags. 'And they call Queen Victoria's England a Christian country,' he thought, 'when there are lads like this roaming about . . . ' He gave John some bread and fat ham, and talked to him about the warmth of the day and the new works on the railway north of the station.

'There's work there, boy, if you want it,' he said gently. John looked up then. It was the first kindly-spoken sentence he had heard in weeks. As he raised his tormented eyes, a group of navvies came in.

There, with a crowd of men, grinning at John, was Handsome Jack.

Far away down the long white road outside the chapel, the Judge in the Assizes Court at Derby was sentencing Jessie. And at that moment John had found Handsome Jack.

CHAPTER
[24]

THE JUDGE was ready in the robing room. He was admiring the new red silk of his robe, fine silk, bought at a cost that would give Mr Rhodes enough money to keep his temperance bar open for two years. Mr Justice Gault admired himself in the long mirror. His expression was the same as Jessie's had been, so long ago, when she had held her blue beads to the moon in her little room under the roof. The red silk caught the April sun from the glass roof and glowed the colour of Jessie's robin's breast. It glowed the colour of blood.

Mr Justice Gault enjoyed the procession into court just as Jessie had enjoyed the procession of John and herself into the churchyard to sledge. Mr Justice Gault held a nosegay of sweet herbs and flowers. He climbed the steps to his huge chair and sat down. His red robe looked like a pool of blood amongst the other people in the court, who wore black gowns, the colour of punishment books and long winter nights without stars.

The Assize opened at ten o'clock. A Grand Jury was sworn in.

Mr Justice Gault gave an opening lecture. He wagged his finger at the lawyers, the clerks, at Mr Grindle-Ford, at Mr Taylor (both in gowns of black), and at the public who had come to see Jessie Smith be sentenced to hang. The number of prisoners in Derby Gaol had increased, Mr Justice Gault said. The crimes were becoming more serious. The criminal classes were getting younger. Mr Justice Gault blamed it on the new Education Bill of fifteen years ago. Children had too much free time to get up to mischief. Well, they would be punished. He would see to that.

There were two cases to be heard before Jessie's, and they were hurried along as when people are impatient to get to a part of a meal that has a rare tit-bit. Jessie was the main meal today.

So a bored court heard about a labourer at Chesterfield who had stolen five shillings after threatening a woman with a knife. That was easily sorted out. The man was given five years hard labour and seven minutes of finger wagging. Then the red silk gown was adjusted, the glasses polished, and the next case heard.

John Varley was accused of stealing a silver watch and chain from Edward Walton of Moonfield Farm near Hartington. It was thought he had stolen a saddle too. He was given three years hard labour, four minutes of finger wagging, and that was that. Now they were all ready for Jessie.

There was almost complete silence as Jessie was brought into court. Almost a silence but not quite. There were faint rustles as necks turned, and slight creakings of bones as people turned to get a better look. There was a slight murmur as she took her seat between two wardresses.

Jessie was stooping a little for she had carried John's great secret for four months now and the burden was heavy. Her face was blank, as though she had just been rescued from drowning in a deep cold underwater cavern. She felt very little. She was numb with misery and cold. It was as well that she did not fully understand what was happening to her.

The Judge, looking at her for the first time, saw a child in a brown prison dress with a pale face and a closed look. 'Sullen,' he thought, and he wrote it down with his gold pencil in his notebook. She had a mean mouth too. The Judge was a big believer in appearances. He thought she looked sly. She would not look up properly. She was round-shouldered too, and would not stand up properly. She looked as if she had done wrong, he thought. He would see to it she was made an example of. There was a long silence while the Judge took in these facts about Jessie. He liked to think that he could 'weigh up' a prisoner by this long stare. He did not like what he saw. Already the scales of justice were weighted against Jessie. The

135

silence grew. It had the quality and bite of the damp cold silence before a long spell of snow arrives in winter. The cold that Jessie had felt within her mind and in the prison was nothing compared to what was coming.

A man in a black gown stood up, and like a winter rook cawing in a snowbound field broke the silence. But the Judge still stared at Jessie. The rook-like man rambled and cawed to the Court, asked a few questions, got no answers, and then read the Charge to Jessie.

'That you, Jessie Smith, aged thirteen years, of New Street in the town of Lambton in Derbyshire, did wilfully, and of your own malice, murder your employer, Ezekiel Dobson on the late evening of the 6th of January, the year of our Lord 1885, in the sacred ground of All Saints churchyard in the said town of Lambton . . . '

There was another wintry frozen silence (still the Judge looked at Jessie, 'taking her in,' he called it) and some more cawing from black-gowned rook-like men. Then the note changed in the rook man's voice. It became harsher, more like the jackdaws that haunted the gargoyles of All Saints Church.

'How do you plead? Guilty or not guilty?' Everyone stared at poor Jessie. She just stared back. The Judge again thought her sullen. Mr Taylor whispered to her through his golden moustache, his breath smelling of port and cigars, his silky moustache close to her prison-grey ear. But she took no notice of him. It meant nothing. His words filtering through the gold hair were as useless as sun in January; nothing could melt the winter frost in the court or in her heart. Only John. John. She stirred a little in her seat. The thought of John made her look up. She heard the whispering around her like snow in a winter wood.

'How do you plead?' croaked the jackdaw man, over and over. But she was thinking of John. She suddenly saw the sea of curious faces like frozen turnips in a frosty field. She saw the panels of the courtroom shining like walls of ice. She was in an ice cavern without John. Fear and horror surged into her. She cringed. She pressed her back against the hard wood of the bench. She felt she was drowning in an icy flood. She began to struggle like a frightened kitten. She scratched and bit the wardresses who held her tight. They held her tight and smacked her down hard. She sobbed and mewed like a captured kitten.

The Judge, who had never taken his eyes off her, leaned forward with an I-told-you-so look in his eyes. He had been watching her closely. He had seen her come in, he thought, thinking she was going to get away with a murder. Then when she had seen him and the Court she had realized she could not get away with doing what she liked. Well, he would show her.

Rook and jackdaw men cawed and chacked at her. She looked wildly round the turnip faces. John . . . where are you?

Despite all the angry caws, Jessie would not plead guilty or not guilty. It meant nothing to her. She was just waiting for John to step forward and then her part was finished.

Because she was taking no notice of the Court, the Judge spoke to her for the first time. He did not like prisoners to take no notice of the Court. It spoiled his own standing, his own dignity. He raised his finger and wagged it.

'Prisoner! You will answer the Court! It is for your own sake that with your own lips you do so. You will, one day, sooner if not later, have to face another Court in Heaven, an even greater Court than the one you are now in. In the Heavenly Court you will face God. But first you have to face me. Speak!'

But Jessie would not. She did not understand what she had to do, and she was scared that if she opened her mouth something would slip out about John letting the stone fall. So she did nothing except make a few heart-rendering mewing noises.

Mr Taylor, furious that Jessie would not stand up and talk, got to his feet. He made a terrible statement for Jessie.

'The prisoner pleads guilty, m'lord.' A sigh went round the courtroom like the east wind blowing through a winter wood. So, she had done it. Jessie Smith was as good as dead. But the statement was a final desperate trick of Mr Taylor to get Jessie out of terible trouble.

Jessie did not realize this. She struggled again and

137

scratched and bit, but she was as feeble as a kitten and they held her there to listen to the constant cawing and crowing. When she was quiet again, she heard Mr Grindle-Ford talking about Throttlepenny to the Court.

'. . . I tell the Court of the sad old gentleman, Mr Ezekiel Dobson, widowed as a young man, a most tragic event and one that must make the Court realize how tragic his death was to be. The old gentleman had led a blameless life. He was a man of hard work. He worked hard and saved hard. It is to such men as Ezekiel Dobson, hard working, thrifty, careful, that we owe the making of our great British Empire. For nearly fifty years this grand old man of Lambton had provided the townsfolk with excellent groceries, fragrant coffees, fine teas, mellow cheeses. I show the Court a kindly, careful old gentleman, busy in his splendid shop, serving the market town of Lambton. A loyal subject to the Queen. Keep this picture in your minds, gentlemen. For now I am going to show you a tearful scene. Picture this grand old man of Lambton. After a hard day in the shop, he shuts it up, and heedless of his own weariness he toils up the long hill of the churchyard to his dear wife's grave. There he kneels a moment in humble prayer. He gently lays on the wintry earth his offering. A bunch of tender snowdrops. He prays again . . . But stay. What happens? A child of vicious intent kills this old man even as he prays, to steal a single gold coin from . . .'

Jessie was trapped in a cold freezing fog of nightmare. What were they talking about? She did not understand. Throttlepenny was a nasty horrid cruel old man. Then why were they saying it? Why? Why didn't John come and tell them it was all wrong?

She struggled like a rabbit trapped in a tangled snare, but they held her down. Mr Grindle-Ford stood there in his black gown, like a spider spinning a web of lies around her. It was a very carefully built web. He had had two months to spin it. Each strand was carefully designed to bind down Jessie, who heard the lies only faintly.

Mr Grindle-Ford made the policeman, P.C. Gratton, describe how he had found the blood-smeared stone, the gold coin in her bedroom, and the little Punishment Book.

That was the centre of the web. It was enough to hold Jessie fast.

For supporting strands, Dr Jones told of the two horrible wounds. Then Mr Grindle-Ford called Mrs Mellor into the Court and she told maliciously how she had seen Jessie pretend to attack the old man in the shop. Mrs Mellor had had a day off from the Workhouse and was going to make Jessie suffer. For more support—for the web must hold Jessie for ever—Mr Grindle-Ford brought in Miss White, Jessie's ex-teacher. 'She was always a deceitful child, laughing in my lessons. She once swallowed a pin to annoy me. That's the type of girl she was.' The web was nearly complete. Mrs Gibbs was called into the witness box next, to tell how she and Fanny had seen Jessie spying on the old man through his keyhole. The web was finished when Fanny was called, to tell how she had seen Jessie running with a stone from the churchyard, and Miss Stardrop told of Jessie's disobedience in letting rats and mice go free in the shop.

But spiders' webs are at their most beautiful in early winter when they are dusted with frost and frozen dew. And Mr Grindle-Ford wanted to decorate his web of lies. It was a cold jewelled web of winter that finally caught Jessie, and Mr Grindle-Ford decorated it with Fanny's evidence. He called her back to the witness box. She looked lovely. She was wearing a white daintily spotted muslin dress, with a yellow sash at her waist exquisitely embroidered with daisies. She wore a white straw hat and a yellow silk scarf. Her blonde curls shone in the hard light of the court. But she was sullen. Her lips were sulky. She pouted. She blushed. She went hot and cold. But she gave evidence. For she still loved John and would not tell what she had seen. She loved him. The picture of him that day with hay in his hair and mud on his boots would not go away. But she hated him too. She had not realized how you could hate anybody so. Now in the witness box, she went hot and cold, hated and loved, felt sorry for Jessie, wept with rage. The Judge thought he had never seen anybody so beautiful and so . . . pure. That was the word he used. So it was Fanny who finished the web. She told of how she had seen Jessie steal the snowdrops in the shop when the old man was not looking.

It was done. All the evidence was collected. Mrs Gibbs sighed. It was over. For days Fanny had said she would not talk in court. One night she had been hysterical and they'd had to smack her. But it was all over now. So Mr Grindle-Ford and everybody thought. But not quite. Like Jessie's love for John, there was a tiny flame of hope left.

Mr Taylor fumed. It was no good asking the little fool Smith to stand up and break the web of lies. But he'd have a go himself to break some of the evidence and save Jessie from dangling on the end of the hangman's rope.

He stood up and spoke to the Judge and Jury. 'M'lord and Gentlemen of the Jury. An hour or two ago I pleaded guilty on behalf of the prisoner. That is because the evidence is so strongly against her. I pleaded guilty for her because she will not speak to me. She is refusing to talk because she is hiding the real truth. I call my first witness, P.C. Gratton.' He was called. Mr Taylor spoke to him.

'It was a snowy night on the night of the murder, Constable? There had been showers all day and in the evening, between sunset and moonrise?'

'Yes, sir.'

'How many footprints around the grave of Mrs Dobson did you see?'

There was a long long silence. The constable cleared his throat. 'I had meant to go back and look, but when we found the stone in the prisoner's yard there did not seem much point, like. It seemed clear cut, like.'

'So you cannot swear to the Court that there were not any other footprints other than Jessie Smith's or Ezekiel Dobson's?'

'No, sir.' Mr Taylor shuffled his papers long enough to let this fact sink into everybody's mind. Then he started again.

'You found a gold sovereign in the prisoner's room when you searched it, did you not?'

'Yes, sir.'

'No more?'

'No more, sir.'

'Yet the old gentleman must have taken, say, about £100 that day in his shop. It was a cold day. People were buying in, fearing cold weather. Yet you found no money in the shop?'

'No, sir.'

'And no money on Mr Dobson's body?'

'About twenty sovs, sir . . . no more though.' There was another silence while Mr Taylor let that fact sink in too. Why steal one coin?

'Thank you, Constable. You may step down.' Mr Taylor shuffled his papers a great deal again to let the Judge and Jury think about all that. Then he called Dr Jones.

'There were two blows on the unfortunate old gentleman's head, Doctor?'

'That is so.'

'Could they have been done by two different people?'

'They could . . . '

Mr Grindle-Ford was on his feet like an angry spider when a bumble bee starts to wreck its web, yet being very careful that it does not get stung.

'But there was not much time between the blows, Doctor?' said Mr Grindle-Ford.

'Very little time.'

'Could there, even if you are not certain, have been, say, a minute between each blow?' Mr Taylor was back, destroying the web.

'Yes, there could . . . possibly. I cannot say.'

'And the lighter blow, that we shall call the first blow, may not have killed him?'

'Possibly. I cannot really say.'

'Thank you, Doctor.'

The cold frosted web holding Jessie was damaged. The Judge became very alert. But he smiled a little as Mr Taylor called for Fanny Gibbs to be brought back into the witness box. He thought Fanny was so pure and beautiful. Mr Taylor smiled at her too. He spoke to her gently.

'You were having a party on the night of the murder, were you not Miss Gibbs?' Fanny smiled for the first time in weeks. She liked the look of Mr Taylor, with his lion-gold hair and silky beard. He smiled back. They liked each

141

other. Fanny decided she liked both rough boys like John and smooth men like Mr Taylor.

'Yes.' Fanny's red lips parted to show her splendid teeth.

'Yet . . . you left your guests to go to the churchyard? . . . Why?'

Fanny blushed a deep red. It made her look prettier than ever. 'I knew many of my other friends had been sledging and thought one or two may have wished to come to my party . . .'

'Who, Miss Gibbs? A young admirer, a boy, perhaps?'

Mr Grindle-Ford was on his feet. 'I do not think m' learned friend has any right to ask such questions of the young lady, m'lord.'

'No, no,' said the Judge, admiring the depth of Fanny's blush. 'But are you quite sure, my dear, you did not see anybody else?'

Fanny looked at the floor. She went hot and cold. She saw John with the hay in his hair in her imagination and she wanted him . . . 'No,' she whispered.

'Thank you,' said Mr Taylor, now quite in love with Fanny himself.

The Judge turned to Jessie with some difficulty after the lovely Miss Gibbs. But he spoke fairly kindly to her, for Mr Taylor had damaged the web.

'Prisoner . . . are you certain you do not wish to say anything to me or the Court?'

But Jessie would not speak. Her pale lips were clamped tight. For she was remembering what John had said to Fanny about not going to the party. And she would never let John down . . . never.

The Judge suddenly rose to his feet. 'The Court is adjourned until ten o'clock tomorrow.'

It was now uncertain whether Mr Grindle-Ford's web would catch Jessie or not.

Outside, the newspapers thought she was caught. A newsgirl, her face as grey and pinched as Jessie's, sold a pile of papers outside the Midland Station. 'SMITH PLEADS GUILTY,' she yelled, her nasal voice ripping into the fresh wind-tossed April sunshine. So Jessie was no longer Jessie. Just Smith.

High up on Lambton Church, the stone devil's eyes gleamed in a passing April shower as it seemed to watch a waggon bring a pile of evening papers down from the station. Perhaps it even saw Emma Briddon buy a copy, for she had been to the apothecary's again.

Sometimes Mr Rhodes was given an old newspaper because he spent all his spare money looking after the poor and homeless. There was a pile in his temperance bar for those who could read to look at. Sometimes it was weeks before the news reached his little chapel.

That night Jessie wept bitterly. Perhaps in her frozen mind she simply realized there was now no escape from this cold hell. She sobbed and screamed and asked the wardress Mrs Sugg for 'the axe'.

'What axe, duck?' asked Mrs Sugg, who had come to love the harmless Jessie. Anyone less like a murderess she could not imagine.

'The axe I took to Mester Dobson's,' she whispered. Mrs Sugg looked at Mrs Mont. There now had to be two wardresses with Jessie, day and night, in case she escaped the final sting of the law. 'That axe were the last thing me dad did for me. I want to touch it because he did.'

'You can't have that, my duck,' said Mrs Sugg, taking the body of Jessie into her arms. Jessie's body was bird light, like a starved wren caught in a winter freeze. She nodded at Mrs Mont. 'There's more to all this than meets the eye,' she said. 'I thought that, when that nice Mr Taylor were asking things this afternoon in court. Are you sure, Jessie m' duck, that you don't want to ask anything, say anything to us?'

But Jessie trembled. More and more she was gripped by the half magic fear that if she opened her mouth the terrible truth about John would come tumbling out. She just wanted the axe.

Mrs Mont said nothing but looked coldly at Jessie. She thought her a poor thing. She could not imagine that poor little thing keeping anything quiet. Later that night, Miss Stenton and another wardress came to relieve Mrs Sugg and Mrs Mont. Jessie now had to have the gas lit all night so that they could watch her. The hissing bright gas had stopped John's visits to her.

Mrs Mont talked in a low voice to Miss Stenton outside the cell door, telling her about the axe. The two women whispered together in the half light, like two wolves on a starlit night planning a kill. They were. Mrs Mont was asking Miss Stenton's advice about the axe. She got the advice.

Five minutes later she was in the Governor's room, writing to the Judge about the fact that Jessie had carried an axe to Ezekiel Dobson's house the night before the murder. Her thin bent body crouched low over the paper as she wrote her message in black ink; writing that was long enough to strengthen the web holding Jessie.

CHAPTER
[25]

THE COURT assembled at ten o'clock.

Mr Justice Gault had read the note. He had been impressed with Mr Taylor. He asked Jessie one more time.

'Prisoner, are you quite certain you are not shielding anyone from this terrible crime? . . . That you do not wish to confess to this Court before it sentences you?'

But Jessie would not say anything. Once again the Judge was angry with Jessie. For some reason she made him feel smaller than he thought he was and he did not like that. He was not used to being ignored. With an angry gesture of the shoulder that made the scarlet silk of his robe shimmer, he turned to the Jury for his summing up.

'You have had before you the police evidence. The stone smeared with blood found in the prisoner's yard. You have heard about the stolen coin. You have heard the good Doctor's evidence about the wounds that killed the blameless old man. You have heard the brave Miss Gibbs doing her duty and testifying against a former classmate. Remember how she described seeing the prisoner running with the stone across the town square. All this is evidence of the most damaging kind.'

'Do not forget the details. Details tell you so much about the whole crime. Do not forget the strange little notebook the prisoner made, which she called a Punishment Book. This in itself proves that violence was always in her mind. Do not forget the stolen snowdrops that she took from the shop. Do not forget that she spied on her employer. I have further evidence that she took a weapon of murder to the house of the old man in the form of an axe. Do not forget Miss

145

Stardrop's account of her disobedience. Do not forget she pretended to attack the old man behind his back.

'But stay! We must put some weight on the opposite side of the scales of justice. All through the case the prisoner has refused to speak to the Court. The Jury must decide whether or not she is witholding important facts that may or may not be to her own advantage. The police did not bother to check the footprints in the snow. There is a chance somebody else delivered the fatal blow and took the money. You must decide whether or not these facts must be taken into account. If you are at all uncertain that the prisoner is guilty, you must say so.

'God be with you in your decision. The Court will now adjourn while the Jury decides its verdict.'

It was the middle of the afternoon before the Jury returned. The Court assembled. A jackdaw man in a black gown spoke to them.

'Gentlemen of the Jury, have you agreed upon your verdict?'

'We have.'

'Do you find the prisoner Jessie Smith guilty or not guilty?'

'Guilty.'

'Is that the verdict of you all?'

'It is.'

The Judge spoke to Jessie. For the first time a look of terror appeared on her frozen grey face. But it was the terror of the rabbit before the weasel. She was paralyzed with fear. No spider injecting a fly could have made it so cold and immobile. She thought of John again . . . Why? Why had he left her?

Fanny too found her teeth chattering. She thought of John. She hated him but she wanted him to live. But the Judge was speaking.

'Jessie Smith, you stand convicted of murder. Is there any reason why I should not pass judgement on you according to the law?' Jessie did not understand what he meant.

'Tell him now, duck,' whispered Mrs Sugg. But Jessie would not tell on John. The Judge asked her again. But her mouth was as clamped now as it had been since January.

Not one person in the Court thought of the word bravery.

The Judge had to let his finger wag for a time. It wagged. He talked.

'You had an education in a new school until you were twelve. Money has been spent on you. That does not give you the right to do as you please. As you seem not to bother speaking to people above you, I shall make an example of you to all the other young people who think they can go around doing as they please.'

A vicar had suddenly appeared beside the Judge. He handed the Judge a square of thick black silk. Despite the remarks about Jessie having had money spent on her, the square of silk cost far more than any of Jessie's clothes ever had. The Judge put the black square of silk on his head.

'Jessie Smith. I sentence you for the murder of Ezekiel Dobson. You shall be taken to the place from whence you came and thence to a place of lawful execution and there you shall be hanged by the neck until you be dead. And afterwards your body shall be buried in a common grave within the precincts of the prison where you were last confined before your execution. May the Lord have mercy on your soul.'

A heart-rending scream filled the court. It was Fanny Gibbs. She stood up and screamed, and then began to laugh and cry. She had never meant this. Or had she? She would have to live with this for ever. Mrs Gibbs hastily waved a cut-glass bottle of smelling salts under Fanny's nose. Fanny screamed again. She hated John for letting this happen to her. She seized the little cut-glass bottle with its silver top and threw it down the gangway of the court, where it fell like a stone glazed with ice in moonlight, like the stone John had dropped. That made her sick.

She was hurried from the court into a horse cab and rushed to the station. In the train she sobbed and screamed to the rise and fall of the telegraph poles. Not until two hours later, after Doctor Jones had given her opium and brandy, did she stop. But then she fell into a tormented sleep. On her way out, she had seen Miss Stenton and Mrs Mont dragging Jessie away. She was reminded of spiders dragging flies into a hole in the garden wall. Fanny dreamed she was sitting in the middle of a wintry world, spinning a web to trap Jessie, a web where she had threaded beautiful beads of ice on the strands. She had shown John the web. Then she had made Jessie get into the web and she couldn't get out, and John would not help, he just ran away. Fanny had the nightmare three times that night. Then she would wake up thinking it was just a nightmare, and not true. But it was true, every bit.

CHAPTER
[26]

JESSIE WAS moved into the Condemned Cell, a special cell for those about to be hanged. It is possible she still did not realize that she was certainly going to die. At thirteen you do not expect to die, and there was still a small glow of light at the back of Jessie's misery and confusion that told her John would come and get her out. The Condemned Cell was slightly more pleasant than where she had been before. There was a small black-leaded fireplace set in the whitewashed wall, but Jessie, though she needed warmth, found that the glow of flames stopped her imagining John.

Mrs Mont and Miss Stenton thought Jessie was a poor mad creature who had not really known what she was doing.

'You can tell by looking at her mother,' Miss Stenton had remarked to Mrs Mont when Jessie's mother and father had come to see her. 'Her mother hardly said a word to her and her father just sat there. She gets her dull wits and poor body from her mother and that obstinate look from her father.' Miss Stenton, with her pointed wolf-like face, had nid-nodded with the bent Mrs Mont. They knew it was just a matter of time till the execution. Jessie had quite rightly and imaginatively called Miss Stenton 'Miss Star' and Mrs Mont 'Mrs Moon'. They were both as cold and remote and uncaring.

Mrs Sugg, whom Jessie called 'Mrs Sun' was a different matter. She saw Jessie for what she really was. She wept a great deal for this pale shy girl who was soon to be executed. She had felt for Jessie's mother, suspecting quite rightly that Jessie's mother was lost without Jessie's help in the home. Mrs Sugg was always wanting to do things for

Jessie. She brought in a rhubarb pie she had made of the finest rhubarb from her own small garden. She made a trip out to a farm and brought in brown eggs, warm and fresh, and let Jessie feel the warmth before she sent them to be cooked. Jessie was extra special now they were going to kill her, and she could have any food she wanted provided somebody brought it in. She let Jessie feel the warmth of the egg against her cold grey cheek. Mrs Sugg realized that Jessie needed warmth. She brought in sunshine coloured humbugs, striped like warm bees, and golden barley sugar sticks that had a little glowing heart of gold in the firelight of the whitewashed cell. But these objects of warmth and light did not work. Jessie was as cold and empty as the frosted shell of a dead fly left in a winter web. She had been sucked dry of all feeling by the non-appearance of John and the spider lies of Mr Grindle-Ford and his prosecution web.

Then three days later, Mrs Sugg had an idea to bring a little warmth and joy to Jessie's life, which already seemed dead before she had been executed. Her daughter Jennie had a three-week-old kitten that gave her endless pleasure. Against all the prison rules and much to Mrs Mont's displeasure—her mouth became the same shape as her bent back—Mrs Sugg smuggled in the tiny kitten for Jessie to play with. It was black, exactly like Smut, her cat back at home. The kitten had big feet with tiny perfect pearl-coloured claws and pink pads under its feet. Its wide and eager eyes were like the shining blue beads that Jessie had left behind in her little attic.

When Jessie saw the kitten dart across the large scrubbed table in the Condemned Cell, the ice-cold grey armour she had fitted round herself since January lifted. This bubble of thin ice she had put around herself was to protect John. The bubble had been sealed with silence. Now the bubble fell apart. Jessie sobbed and sobbed. Not the fearful shuddering sobs of fear and frustration and bewilderment she had produced before. These were sobs for life that she wanted so badly to live. To see the robin come for crumbs on a winter morning, to feel the soft skin and soft hair of her young brothers, and most of all to have Smut come through her attic window to sleep with her. It was light and warmth and life she cried for. The kitten scuttled across the table, its claws rattling, patting, pawing, jumping, leaping on to a piece of paper screwed up and fastened to a string. Then it became tired, fanned its claws for a few seconds, then nestled up to Jessie and began a moth-like whirring that was a baby purr. 'John . . . ,' sobbed Jessie, 'Oh John, why don't you come?'

'John who, my little duck?' soothed Mrs Sugg. She was wisely letting Jessie cry on. She knew the difference between healing tears and bitter tears, and these were healing. If only she could make the poor little lass happy for her last few weeks.

'John Mellor, my sweetheart,' said Jessie, relaxed and uncaring now, as she had not been since January. 'He said he'd get me out and he never has.' Jessie was now mixing fact and fantasy from those long imaginary moonlight visits of John. Mrs Sugg said nothing more to Jessie, but they fed the kitten when it awoke and talked of cats they had known.

'Oh, there's more to all this than meets the eye,' said Mrs Sugg when she got home. 'I'd like to meet this John, that I would.'

Mrs Sugg was not a woman to let matters stand idle. The following Monday was her day off, and she packed her Gladstone bag with food and caught a train from Derby Station to Lambton. It was a lovely April day and Mrs Sugg would have enjoyed the ride greatly, but it was spoiled thinking of that poor young girl waiting to die.

'It's not right you know!' she said out loud several times, to the astonishment of the other travellers in the third-class compartment. They wondered why this stout lady dressed in black kept saying this whenever she saw a field with lambs racing in it, or when the station cat at Matlock was seen asleep in a pool of sun, or when a gentle April shower and a soft rainbow appeared over the hills and spire of Lambton, as the carriage rocked and swayed towards the town.

Mrs Sugg had her dinner by the river and fed the ducks. Then, duck's head umbrella gripped under her stout arm, she went to look for 'this John'. But she could not find him.

She bought a tablet of wallflower-scented soap from the apothecary; seeing a thin pale woman buying a large quantity and talking to the man, she thought she would do the same. The man looked like a gossip. She was right. He told her John Mellor had not been seen since the day of the first trial. He told her some very unpleasant things about John. He couldn't keep a job, had been seen drunk and swearing on the highroads, slept in barns and was looking for girls to get into trouble. Mrs Sugg sniffed as she left the shop. She'd like to get her hands on this young man, she thought.

She went to Jessie's mother but could get no sense. The cottage was in chaos. There were pails of dirty washing, the fire was choked, a thin mangy tom cat mewed for food, the babies cried, and Mrs Smith cried. No, she hadn't seen John Mellor.

Mrs Sugg toiled up the hill to the station in a shower of soft rain that pattered on her brolly and the new leaves. She paused for breath half-way up and looked back. Her long-sighted eyes looked across to the churchyard in the distance. She sighed. That little thing Jessie murdering some old man. She could not believe it. A rainbow leaped from the dark clouds and ended in the churchyard. A blackbird sang. In the great woods above the station a cuckoo shouted. Mrs Sugg saw it as a sign.

'It'll be all right, Jess, m' duck,' she said aloud to some black-nosed lambs looking at her through the fiery green mist of the hawthorn hedge. 'It'll be all right. Just let me get my hands on that John Mellor. An' I will an' all, or else my name's not Dolly Sugg.'

CHAPTER
[27]

HANDSOME JACK had drunk some tea and coffee and grinned at John. John did not know whether it was a smile of recognition or whether there was some evil thinking behind it. For the moment he did not care. The navvyman went on drinking his tea then suddenly stared at John again. He got up and threw the big pot mug the length of the little room at the back of the chapel. The mug rolled and smashed. There was silence for a time as navvies, Mr Rhodes and John stared at the fragments which were like fallen white rose petals. Then Handsome Jack roared, 'Dang an' blast ye all . . . ' Then he stormed out of the room, banging the door loudly.

'Has Jack been drinking again?' Mr Rhodes calmly asked the navvies.

'Worse than ever, Mester Rhodes,' said one. 'He seems to have endless brass for togs and booze. Where he gets it all from none of us knows . . . but you can't talk to him these days he's so foul tempered . . .'

Mr Rhodes nodded then turned his attention to looking after John. He gave the utterly exhausted boy more hot sweet tea and more bread and fat ham. Then when John had recovered, he offered to take him across to the navvies' camp to get him a job. John agreed wearily. It was the last thing he wanted. He just wanted to run away from all his cowardice and kill himself. But that wasn't to be.

John got work as usual, backed up by Mr Rhodes' kind words and his own size. As usual they were glad of a strong lad who would not need full wages but could do the full day's work of a grown man. John looked round him. After the tea and food, the little voice was getting ready to get at him again, he knew. It was not a big shanty town. John had seen much bigger ones when he was looking round the railways. Here were just a few huts in a mirror-like sea of mud, with planks for paths leading to them. The High Peak line had taken on the men to straighten out a half mile of S-bend in the old track which they were upgrading. There was about a year's work here in this lonely cold spot. A marvellous place to hide from the world for both John and Handsome Jack.

John set to work, doing his usual job of wheeling barrowful after barrowful of soil and rubble from the new cutting to the new embankment. It was a grey day, with snow in the air now. The warm sun of the morning had given way to what the locals called a 'lambing storm'. During one of the thicker whirling snow flurries, John turned. There was a man watching him. It was the navvyman, Handsome Jack. He did not appear to be working. He was leaning against some new fencing, smoking his short clay pipe and just watching John. He was dressed as smartly as ever with jacket, waistcoat, high-laced boots, and spotted necktie. John felt the same as he had done before. One bit of him admired the man. Another part warned him of danger. As Jack continued to watch him, John felt shivers of fear stroke his spine. Matters were going to come to a head soon. Well, he told himself angrily, he didn't care. He may as well be dead. He could not live with himself much longer.

John was now suffering a numbness like Jessie. He had been in the cold emptiness of the last few months for too long. His feelings were freezing now. Even the little nagging voice that so tormented him was becoming muffled and distant, like a stream that is slowly freezing in a hard winter. John could not take much more.

'Ask Handsome Jack tonight what he knows,' said the little voice in its now muffled voice. 'But watch him . . . watch him . . . don't be with him alone. He could kill you for what you know . . . but you'll have to, if Jessie is to be saved.' John sent a barrowload of stones rattling down the tip in a fury. Handsome Jack saw him do it too.

But he did not kill John that night. Neither was John able

to speak to him. After watching John for an unnerving three hours, Jack went off and became blind drunk. There were three camp fires that night, and he lurched from one to the other, roaring out songs and oaths that awoke the plovers on those high hills. He became louder and louder as the night wore on. John cowered under a hut, protected from the north-west wind and warmed by the fire. He kept close by the other navvies who laughed at Jack and took such wild behaviour for granted. All the navvies went wild like this from time to time. They saw nothing strange in it. Even when Jack's bellowing and belches became loud enough to make a horse and carriage swerve on a road three fields away, they took no notice. He smashed in the side of a hut with his bare fists and shouted at the moon. John lay staring at the fire and thinking, 'I bet he thought I was in that hut . . . '

'Got summat on his mind, I reckon,' said one navvy at last in the little group John was trying to hide with.

When he followed the men into a hut and lay down in the straw, he could see Jack through the open door. In the grey and white moonlight and thin snow, John could see him propped up against a hut, weeping and whimpering. But John did not dare go over to the giant. He was glad when the men shut the door on the moonlight and the sobbing man. Even the little voice did not expect him to go over to Jack. John did not know just how urgent his mission was, or else it might have done.

The next day was, though John did not know it, the one on which Jessie was sentenced to death.

Handsome Jack still stared at John, and the other men began to notice it.

'Does old Jack know thee, lad?' asked one of the men, who was supervising where John and the others were tipping their rubble.

'I worked with him once,' said John.

'Keep out'n his way lad, while the booze is still in him,' said the other wisely. John made certain that he did. The strange looks he got from Jack made him want to leave the camp, but the half frozen little voice said no, he must stay. The little voice did not know that Jessie had less than three weeks to live.

A week later John had made no progress. He had not dared approach the navvy. On the other hand, the navvy had done nothing to John. John was caught up in the hard routine of labouring and the little voice was not as strong as it had been; it was so easy to forget what was going on in the world on these high hills.

John was wheeling his barrow one afternoon, his body bent into the stiff cold north-westerly wind, the sun hot on his back. It had been a perfect late April day. The sky was pure blue with the sun high and warm like a vast dandelion of hot gold. It seemed supported there by a net of larksong. The men whistled as they walked around the net of endless white limestone walls on ground dusted with the lesser suns of a million celandines. John and Handsome Jack did not whistle, but like the rest of the men they screwed up their eyes against the dust the wind blew from the mounds of earth into their faces.

A particularly sharp gust tossed the larks, whirled the dust in spirals, and blew a newspaper from the turnpike road four fields away. The newspaper was smeared with grease from a limecarter's bread and bacon dinner, but one of the men picked it up.

'Go on, then, read it to us, clever bugger,' John heard Jack say in his loud voice.

The man with the newspaper must have been one of the few men on the camp who could read. John had kept the fact to himself that he could read and write quite well, and had once, hundreds of years ago it now seemed, ridden on the Duchess of Derbyshire's coach . . .

John could not hear what was said. But after some minutes he saw Jack reel and stagger away to a hut and bang the plank door. The reader shrugged his shoulders and chucked the paper down, and went on with his wheeling, for the foreman was watching. On his way back from the tip, the wind blew the paper to John and he picked it up.

JESSIE SMITH WILL HANG—AGE MAKES NO DIFFERENCE JUDGE SAYS—CRUEL MURDER MUST BE PUNISHED

John read it and the world darkened and spun around him. The paper was a week old. He read, as though looking through the wrong end of a telescope, that Mr Taylor and the Judge had agreed that there should be a three week wait for execution, as there were some 'slight discrepancies in the evidence, that should be examined before her death'. Her death. Her death. He could not believe it. He worked the rest of the day in a daze, a dream of sick horror. His worst imaginings had come true.

He took little notice of the fact that Handsome Jack was drunk again by sunset and knocking-off time. While the other men were eating their meat round the fire, Handsome Jack came and vomited into the flames.

'He'll kill himself,' said a man near to John. 'He only works one day in five. Where he gets his brass from nobody knows.' John said nothing, but threw his food into the bright fire. There was always plenty of good meat in the camps, the men being encouraged to spend their high wages on beef and steak every night from the tommy shop. John could not eat anything tonight.

He went to his straw at nine o'clock, sick with himself and for Jessie. He was calm now and deeply depressed. He was a coward, a hopeless coward. He lay in the straw staring at the stars through gaps in the roof, but not seeing them. He just wanted to die, but he had not the courage to do that either . . .

At five o'clock the next morning a tremendous banging began. The other men slept on. Many slept through drunken riots. John sat up wearily. Through the banging he could hear the sound of a man crying. John peeped out.

The sun was rising in a halo of cold gold. In front of the sunrise, the navvies' spades were stuck into a mound of earth, the handles silver with dew, so that the mound looked like the stamens of a giant gold and silver flower. The sky was the incredible blue of hill country. Invisible larks were singing and a full moon of honeyed gold swam in

157

the west. It was a morning for miracles. Nothing short of a miracle could save either Jessie's life or John's bleak and miserable existence.

John could see Handsome Jack stark naked, smashing in a barrel. John shuddered. Not at the nakedness, he'd seen so much of that now, but at the wild animal power of the man. He was like a giant-muscled reptile. Like many of the navvies, his body was covered in a fine layer of thin mud, and as he flexed his great muscles the covering cracked into reptile-like scales. John stared. The man was a giant devil, golden in the cold sunlight of the morning world, smashing his great fists down as he had, most likely, in the churchyard. If only there was proof, if only he could save Jess.

Another navvy had awakened and was sitting propped up on an elbow in the straw, yawning, scratching, watching John watch Handsome Jack.

'Keep away, Ginger,' he said to John. John had been accepted by the men—as soon as you were, you got a nickname. 'Keep away, Ginger. He's going barmy. Drink's poisoned him, see? Talking of devils he's seen, he is. Devils that murder, he says. Only devils he'll see are in his own mind from drink. Keep away, Ginger.'

John did. But it was an exquisite day. A day for miracles.

The men must have caught the beauty of the day, for at night they built one big fire and all the men sat round it, as the primitive people who once lived on these high uplands might have done. The men ate and drank slowly and carefully. There seemed a magic in the air. Perhaps it was the full moon that climbed up slowly to the east, brilliantly silver over the gold of the fire.

Handsome Jack walked slowly over to John and sprawled by his side. John felt a shiver tingle through him. Handsome Jack was carrying a chicken he had stolen and he began to pluck it, tossing the feathers into the fire where they burned and rose as ghostly fragments of gold towards the moon. Then Jack scooped out the chicken's guts, his hands covered in blood in the moonlight. John felt again the tingle and shiver of fear that this man always gave him.

Jack did not want the guts and he tossed them into the fire. Then he put the chicken on a sleeper nail and roasted it, staring at John as he did so.

The man who had warned John earlier got up to go to the straw. He whispered in John's ear as he clambered up. 'Watch him, lad. I should gerrin now.'

But John did not. John had been very harsh on himself. He knew he had not the courage to own up and say that he had dropped the first stone. He knew he might be hanged in Jessie's place. But tonight he did have courage. He stayed by the half crazed giant's side until there was only himself and Handsome Jack by the cone of glowing ashes. If Jack killed him, so be it. John was shaking with fear. He knew he must stay. He did not even need the little voice to tell him that. He stayed. Then Handsome Jack made a move towards him.

'I telled thee I'd tell thee a story when the time were right,' he said softly, settling himself uncomfortably close to John, who felt wave after wave of shivers creep up his back. 'Well, it's time, lad. I were in Lambton churchyard on the night that owd feller were done in, you know the story. They're going to hang a little lass for it . . . ' As if John needed telling that.

The fire shifted and sank with a whisper. The navvy tore a strip of steak, threaded it through the thirty-inch nail and held it to the fire where it began to sizzle. His hands were red with chicken blood and firelight. John stared and stared and shivered. Jack's face was red in the firelight, but his moleskin waistcoat was silvered at the back with moonlight. He looked half human, magical. John held his breath, half expecting to feel the fiery point of a knife in his back, or those great hands round his neck. He waited. An owl called, far away down the valley of the River Dove. It was so quiet you could hear an express whistling as it charged down the Midland Line, four miles to the east.

'I thought I'd spend the night in the church porch,' said Jack softly. 'I were sick of mucky workhouses an' being bossed about . . . '

John said nothing. Would he kill him with those bloody

159

hands when he had finished his story? 'There you go again, fearing for yourself,' said the little voice. 'Listen to what he's saying and see if it'll save Jess.'

'... I'd taken me bread and cheese in, like,' the navvyman was saying, 'and I were getting ready to settle down. I thought I'd just have a last pee against a gravestone, all respectable like, when I hears this laugh. Well, I looks up like, an' right above me there's this stone devil carving, laughing at me.' John shivered. He remembered Jessie's ghost stories but he had never heard them told like this. The navvyman was staring into the fire, John forgotten so it seemed. His handsome face was creased into a half smile. He told the tale almost dreamily. John edged away and threw a small branch into the embers. The frosted dew on it hissed and spat.

'... well, I stares like, at this laughing stone face. I'd not been drinking. Well, not much, anyway. I remembered thinking it might have been an owl, but I've heard owls an' this were a proper laugh.' He turned to John and stared at him. John felt butterflies in his stomach. Then the navvy looked back to the blazing branch. 'Well, I were standing there looking up at this devil's face on the church wall, when I hears this rustle, like a snake in dry grass. So I looks round. There were this figure like, in a black cloak wi' a white skellyton face in the moonlight. It were a night like this, you know.' John nodded. Would he ever forget?

'Its face were made of bone. Bare bone. It stood and stared at me and then this thing laughed at me. Then it beckons wi' its finger like. It had hands made out o' shadows ... ' Handsome Jack paused. He was a good storyteller and he wanted to see that John was listening. Again he edged closer to John, and again John felt a delta of shivers form on his back.

'I had to follow, lad. I had to. Anyhow, this devil or whatever it were led me to this old feller kneeling by a grave. He'd got one hand to his head, an' he were putting some flowers on grave. Then this devil creature creeps up on him and it laughs again, just like the one on church wall had ... Then this devil bends slowly an' picks up a stone an' clouts the old feller over his head with it. Well, the owd man falls down like. I were just stood there. This devil wipes the stone on its shadow hands and throws it in snow . . . Well, I reckon it must have been that man Dobson, who they say that young lass did in. You see, Ginger, I reckon that devil did it . . . but who'd believe me?' John said nothing. There was so much to take in.

'Anyway, it laughs again. I can hear it now. That's one reason why I've been drinking so much . . . Then it points to the old man on the ground and bends over him and shakes the body. It pulled at the coat pocket and this great pile o' gold coins fell into snow. Well, devil kept pointing at the gold as if it wanted me to pick it up, so I did. Well, you would, wouldn't you? Then I went back for me pack, an' ran for my bloody life.'

So that was it. John believed him utterly. It fitted in with all Jessie's stories. He and Jessie had once been attacked by an unseen presence in the woods and John believed in tales like this. He had no doubt the navvy told the truth.

Handsome Jack suddenly began to cry. 'They'll hang that young lass, they'll hang her.'

'We'll have to stop them,' said John simply. It was a brave thing to say because he still had a strange animal fear of the man. 'Will you come to Lambton tomorrow and we'll see this Mr Taylor who were on Jessie's side, an' you can tell him the truth?'

Handsome Jack just nodded and then ate slowly. After a while, John found himself helping the man to his hut, watching him go in and then closing the door. He felt like a person who has just seen a man-eating lion back to its cage. He spent the rest of the night wide awake, expecting Handsome Jack to loom up and kill him now he knew his secret.

CHAPTER
[28]

BUT HANDSOME Jack did not kill John that night. Next
morning when John joined the men in the breakfast line, he
was there waiting for bread, hot bacon and a tin mug full of
hot coffee laced with crude rum. He looked like a man who
had put down a great burden. He looked younger. He had
taken the trouble to shave himself. John was wearily
suspicious but past caring. The little voice was silent. For
the moment John could do no more than take the
navvyman to Lambton, where they could both tell the
truth. As he sipped the hot fiery coffee that breathed fumes
of hot cheap rum into his brain, the little voice warned him
that the road down to Lambton was a long and lonely one
and the morning was misty. A lot could happen.

John smiled grimly as they walked away together from
the shanty town. How many times had he turned his back
on work in the last few months? He had lost count. They
crossed the fields with their heads down looking at the
frosty dew, each wrapped in his own thoughts. Handsome
Jack was unusually quiet. He said not a word as they
crossed the second field and John felt a wave of shivery fear
again. The mist swirled around them. It matched their
moods. Now and again, over the endless limestone walls, a
hawthorn tree loomed up; a fiery mist of green, dripping
large drops of dew on them both. After the third tree had
loomed up like this, Handsome Jack spoke. They had
reached the edge of the road.

'Wait lad. Just got to see a man about a dog.' He walked
away in the direction of Moonfields Farm and vanished.
John was left desolate. He felt like a child abandoned by a

parent in the fog. In fact a tear trickled down his dirty cheek like the dew from the hawthorn behind him. He waited and he waited. He kept turning and his tired eyes kept trying to look through the mist. He felt that any moment he might feel those blood-stained hands around his neck. Strangely, the navvyman had shaved but had not washed the chicken's blood off his hands.

In the distance a cockerel crowed. Once . . . twice . . . then a third time. A cart laden with lime clattered by. A train chugged slowly towards the navvy camp loaded with building materials. John smelled the sulphur in the air from its smoke and steam, although he could not see it. A skylark rose in the mist. A weasel poked its head out of the stone wall. Nobody came. John wanted to run but knew that Jack was his only hope. In the end he sat in the ditch against the wall and put his head in his hands. Everything had gone wrong . . . and this was what poor Jess would be feeling, only a thousand times worse. And he was to blame.

He nearly leaped into the air when he felt a firm touch on his shoulder. It was Handsome Jack standing and grinning at him in the first rays of the struggling sun. John stared, suddenly ashamed of the wetness on his cheek. John had never feared or admired anybody quite so much.

'Just thought I'd hide some of that devil's gold,' said Jack. 'We'll keep quiet about how much I took, shall we?' He had hidden a quantity of gold sovereigns behind the bricks of a disused pigsty at Moonfield Farm where he had once worked. John nodded. It did not interest him. All he wanted to do was save Jessie. Jack gave John two gold sovereigns. John took them saying nothing. They would do for his mother. When Jessie was rescued he would get his mother out of the Workhouse. He still felt bad about that. Then he thought no more. He was too exhausted to think about the consequences of what he was doing.

They got a lift on a cart carrying coals. Handsome Jack was in high spirits and whistled as he rode at the back of the long flat cart. He stretched in the sun like a contented cat. They got into Blackdon Square at ten o'clock, just as the bells were striking the hour close by the gargoyle's head.

John had read in the paper that Mr Taylor was helping

Jessie and he knew where the office of the lawyer was. John stared around him as they made their way to the lawyer's. Lambton seemed a lost paradise. The Square was golden in the April sunshine. A dog was sitting in the middle, his tongue hanging out. A hen had strayed into the centre and was scratching in some horse dung. A pony and trap stood outside the watchmaker's. Handsome Jack followed John into the office.

A young man stared at them rudely. He sat on a high stool with a padded leather cushion nailed to it. He picked his teeth with the end of a quill as John asked to see Mr Taylor on urgent business. The young clerk kept them waiting a whole hour. He did not hold with such tramps as this having business with his Mr Taylor. Whatever it was could be of little importance. Tramps like this had nothing important in their lives. So John and Handsome Jack sat on a hard bench in the shadows, a place where the messenger boys and postmen put their parcels and letters. Ladies and gentlemen on important business waited in a pleasant room that overlooked a little garden and the Square. The clerk had decided that the two tramps were of no importance whatsoever.

Eventually the clerk decided to pick up a speaking tube that was connected to Mr Taylor. He put the tortoiseshell horn mouthpiece to his sneering lips.

'What's your names?' he asked with a scowl.

'John Mellor,' said John. To think he had once ridden past this youth high on the Duchess's carriage.

'Jack,' said Handsome Jack with a grin.

'John Mellor and Jack to see you, Mr Taylor,' said the clerk. He fully expected to be able to tell them there was no chance of them being seen. There was an explosion of sound down the tube from Mr Taylor that startled the clerk. Then there was the sound of a door being opened on the floor above and the sound of footsteps on the wooden stairs. Mr Taylor stood in front of them. So! His dreams had come true.

'Come upstairs, will you?'

The clerk was astounded and began to try and restore his view of the tramps. 'Mr Taylor, sir, you have Miss Briddon

164

at eleven. You have old Mrs Walton at half past. At twelve you are seeing Dr Jones. Then you have to discuss Thursday's auction. You are seeing the Archdeacon over lunch.' Tramps must be put in their place. Mr Taylor flicked out his gold watch like a snake's tongue.

'Quickly. Upstairs. State your business.'

'We can tell you who did the murder,' said John.

'Yes?' said Mr Taylor with snake-like eye.

'It were this stone devil like . . .' John had said it.

Mr Taylor blinked the watchful snake eye. 'This is not a laughing matter. Have you been drinking, Mellor?' There was silence.

'We're not joking. We want to tell you the truth. It was a devil.' Mr Taylor stared at them. What a pair of layabouts they looked. Up to no good, that was certain. A devil indeed! It was not even a clever story. But they might be worth talking to. If he could lure them into saying something, he might yet get Jessie saved. And if he could get these two hanged, the world would be a better place. Getting Jessie off would do him a lot of good as a lawyer. Out came the watch as fast as a reptile's tongue catching careless flies.

'Very well. I'll see you after my luncheon. Two, sharp.' Then he thought. What if they go? The very last chance for Smith would be lost. But any fool that expected him to believe a story about stone devils doing murders would not be likely to run away.

'Will you be staying in Lambton till two o'clock?'

'Yes,' said Handsome Jack grandly. 'I've got money for us dinner at Anchor Inn.'

'I'm sure you have,' said Mr Taylor with sun-warmed snake smoothness. The sooner you two are dangling on the hangman's rope the better, he thought.

Mr Taylor was right. John and Jack did not go. Jack went to the Anchor Inn and ordered oxtail soup, beef and potato pie, plum pudding and a Hartington cheese for himself and John. He also ordered a bottle of port and two mugs of best Derby ale. They ate solidly and with enjoyment and were

165

just about ready for Mr Taylor at two o'clock. Mr Taylor was very glad to see them. He had cursed himself through a very boring lunch with Dr Ball, the Archdeacon, for letting them go.

First of all he listened. He kept them both standing in front of his desk, a sure sign of what he thought about them; but John and Jack were used to being pushed around and did not notice the insult. Mr Taylor was unconsciously rude the whole time they talked. He poured a glass of port for himself and did not offer them a glass. Usually his clients were offered a glass of sherry or port wine and a sugar biscuit on a silver tray. He let the hot sun of late April beat down through the glass on to their heads. Usually there was a lot of fiddling with the linen blinds before he began his smooth talk.

John began with how he had climbed up the tower. He told how the stone had fallen from the damaged carving. But only one stone fell. Jessie must have picked up that first stone and run with it to save him. A tear, much to his great shame, trickled down his filthy face for the second time that day. Mr Taylor leaned back in his sun-warmed chair of fine green leather. He arranged his silver inkwell. He moved the little walnut boat-shaped blotter. He looked at John's long matted greasy red hair. His ears were black inside. His eyes were shining as he told his story. Mr Taylor thought he had never seen anyone who looked more like a criminal. John's shirt collar had long since vanished and his shirt was stiff with food and grease stains. His trousers were torn and tied at the knees with twine. One of the toes of his boots flapped open.

Handsome Jack then told him how the devil had led him to Throttlepenny and then killed the old man. He told the story well. Mr Taylor stared as he talked. He looked at the peaked cap set at a rakish angle. Ignorant man, thought Mr Taylor, to keep his cap on while I'm listening. He looked at the silk necktie, in dreadful taste. The fellow had probably bought it in a fairground. The man's hands were filthy, with blood round the wrists . . . Mr Taylor looked at the moleskin waistcoat and the cheap shining brass watch chain. He looked at the big wide belt with its large brass

166

buckle. He took in the fancy high-laced working boots. The man was a lout. The sooner the world was rid of this type of creature the better.

Mr Taylor stood up. He did not want them to see his amazement that they thought he might, for one minute, believe such a story as this. There was certainly enough here to get a reprieve for Jessie Smith. Then he would see to it that these two were hanged. He walked over to the window and stood rudely with his back to them. He poured himself some more wine. He looked out. The window had a glorious view. He looked out over rooftops to fold after fold of wooded hill, blue misted with April heat, green misted with spring, where the river, a golden thread, wound its way to the distant Castle. Mr Taylor had a great deal in life, and this view too. He looked down into the Square below.

In the Square he could see that lovely young girl, Miss Fanny Gibbs, practising with the schoolchildren for May Day. He waved down to her. She waved back but he could see she was not enjoying life. She was angry with the children, almost shouting at them. He saw her smack the legs of two little boys and the face of an older girl. The poor girl had been so dreadfully upset by the Case. Then he made one of his snake-like movements, whiplashing back on John and Jack. He asked them to tell their stories again, and was surprised that they told them exactly the same. He had not expected that. When people told a pack of lies they usually let one lie slip.

He quickly wrote some notes and cancelled all his appointments for the rest of the day and tomorrow. Then he brought parchment and pens. The clerk was called and he came clattering up. Only then did Mr Taylor ask John and Jack to sit down. The clerk put a piece of old newspaper on John's chair.

Then the clerk wrote down exactly what they said as John and Jack told their stories a third time. Again Mr Taylor marvelled that they said it exactly the same. Mr Taylor told them he was making their stories into an affidavit which could be read in a Court. John and Jack had to swear on the Bible. Then Mr Taylor read their stories to them and asked if they would like to change them. They would not. Then Mr Taylor signed the stories. Then the clerk did. Then the clerk put some fancy red sealing wax on the document and John and Jack had to sign.

'Can you write?' Mr Taylor asked John. He nodded. He signed his story in the fine copperplate he had been taught at school. Mr Taylor stared. He had not expected the writing to be better than his own. But the navvy could only make a cross on the paper and Mr Taylor's faith in tramps was restored. Mr Taylor was glad it was done. He would not rest until these rogues were in prison.

'I shall now go to London to see the Home Secretary in person,' said Mr Taylor, 'to get Jessie Smith reprieved from hanging.' John's dirty face shone with joy. You wait, young-fellow-me-lad, thought Mr Taylor. 'Will you be staying in Lambton? . . . the Workhouse will have you.'

'Us'll go and stay at the Anchor until we're needed,' said Handsome Jack. Again Mr Taylor stared. Never had two fools fallen so neatly into the hands of the law.

'Ah . . . yes . . . How much, er, Jack, did you say fell out of the late Mr Dobson's pocket when the . . . er . . . devil . . . attacked him?'

'Just a sov, as I said,' said Handsome Jack without a flicker of an eyelid.

'Ah . . . yes. I forgot you stated that in the affidavit.' He watched them both go. There was a rumble of thunder as he put the affidavits in a case. The sky had suddenly darkened. Poor Miss Gibbs. Her fun would be spoiled. The thunder rumbled again like a distant avalanche waiting to crush John and Jack.

Mr Taylor ran up Station Road. There was no time to wait for a carriage or a cab. The thought that he was ridding the world of a useless lout of a boy and a big ignorant navvy gave him energy. He was out of breath when he reached the station yard. Thunder rumbled, closer now.

'Ah, Baker,' said Mr Taylor to the Station Master. 'Could you flag down the five ten Pullman from Manchester to London? I know it does not stop here, but I know you stop it sometimes for the Duchess.'

'Well, sir, you'll have to pay dear for it if I do. The Company don't like it, you know.'

'It is a matter of life and death.'

Mr Taylor waited on Platform 2 while hail and rain lashed the iron and glass canopy. Soon afterwards the Station Master waved to a halt with a red flag the London express, and to a screech of brakes and steam Mr Taylor climbed into a first-class carriage, giving the angry guard on the train a half sovereign trip. Miss Briddon would pay. He was so pleased with himself that when the train stopped at Derby he went to the dining carriage and ordered dinner and a bottle of champagne. Miss Briddon would pay. He was at St. Pancras by eight o'clock, booking himself into a suite of rooms and explaining why he had no luggage.

At nine o'clock the next morning he took a cab to Whitehall.

As eleven o'clock was striking on Big Ben, he was seeing the Home Secretary.

By four o'clock Queen Victoria had signed Jessie's reprieve from hanging. But Jessie was not to be let out. She was to be detained at Her Majesty's pleasure until such time as there should be a second trial to find out who were the murderers of Ezekiel Dobson.

The thunder storm had been a long one. It had rolled round and round the Derbyshire hills, and the gargoyle had chuckled and spluttered all through it. It had spoiled Fanny Gibbs's plans once more. She had wanted to practise the May Day dances again.

Torrential rain, mixed with sleet and hail, had covered the bluebells and primroses with a cold wet slime of winter and they looked as if they would never recover. But when the spring sun shone on the bluebell wood that afternoon it was as if the storm had never been.

Mrs Sugg told Jessie the news soon afterwards. So the iron grey bubble fell away from Jessie, just as the snow and sleet had melted on the spring flowers in the far-off woods of home. Mrs Sugg thought she had never seen anything so lovely as Jessie's pale elfin face when she heard that she had been reprieved because John and another man had been to the lawyer.

Later that night the moon shone on bluebell wood. It rose late but when it shone it showed the recovered flowers in its silver brilliance. It shone in Jessie's cell. Miss Stenton who was outside heard Jessie cry out. Looking in, she saw the girl hold out her arms to the moonlight. 'I knew you'd come,' she heard her say. 'I'm all right now John. But are you?' Miss Stenton snorted. She had always known Jessie was half mad.

Handsome Jack and John were arrested at eight o'clock in the Anchor Inn, Lambton. They were taken by special train to Derby. John did nothing to save himself. He saw no reason to, as he was telling the truth. As for Handsome Jack, he struggled a bit but, like John, he thought he was telling the truth; well, almost the truth.

A great peace had descended on John. Jessie had been saved. The little voice slept. John slept in his cell at Derby Gaol as he had not slept since his time at Blackdon Castle.

Neither John nor Jack realized that Mr Taylor was sitting at his desk along with other lawyers, who were rustling their papers like the dry coils of a snake. For just as the Punishment Book had columns for punishment if children did anything wrong at school, so the law must take somebody to the gallows. Mr Taylor hoped it would be both John and the navvyman.

It was the same courtroom in Derby. But things had changed. Sunlight cascaded in through the glass light in the roof. It had been a deep ice cave of a place when the Judge had sentenced Jessie to death. But now it was hot. It was stifling. The sun poured into the court and filled it up with more and more light and heat. Before, the court had seemed like a desolate winter field. Today, it seemed like a snake pit with rustlings and slitherings, whisperings and hissings, and Mr Taylor whispering about John in a dry voice through the heat.

Before the new trial in this pit of heat and sun, the lawyers had done a great deal of talking. They had talked to John in his cell. They had talked to Jessie in her new cell, and Jessie had talked back, for now she knew John had come to rescue her. But they were not allowed to see each other. Jessie liked her new cell. It had whitewashed walls where the sun made moving patterns of leaves from a giant horse chestnut outside the prison. She was certain all would be well. The lawyers had been to Lambton to see Fanny Gibbs, and Fanny had had to come to Court again and miss her dancing. Now they were all here for a new trial, and Mr Taylor looked at John with his snake-like eyes and fidgeted in his hot black gown.

The lawyers still looked like big black rooks, but now they were sleepy rooks basking in the sandy coloured pit of golden sun that was the courtroom. It was still the Easter Assizes but there was a different Judge this time. Today Mr Justice Sparrow was going to try the murderers of Ezekiel Dobson. He was a small perky man with thin black bouncy legs that walked quickly into the courtroom in their black silk stockings and buckled shoes. His robes were a little short and the legs moved fast like a small bird taking its perch in a tree. But he was a different man from Mr Justice Gault. Everybody thought he looked a kind man. But he was not. He had every intention of hanging somebody. His eyes twinkled like summer stars behind his round gold glasses, twin summer ponds reflecting the hot sun. But now he smiled. Mr Taylor smiled. And the man who was going to prosecute the defendant smiled. He was Sir Rudyard Warmley Q.C., a very famous man. Today there were going to be no mistakes. This time the defendant would hang.

For the moment Sir Rudyard did not seem to be prosecuting anybody. He held his gown and blinked like a sun-saturated rook, and his voice was as soft as a snake rustle in the warmth. He smiled at John as though he were a long-lost servant. He talked to John for some time as he would to a fierce stray dog that he wanted to catch and get out of the way. He seemed almost to be offering John tempting morsels to catch him.

'So,' said Sir Rudyard, blinking in the dazzle, 'you ran into All Saints Church and hid, and climbed up the tower to escape the chastisement of the good Doctor Ball. Doctor Ball has sworn to seeing, to the best of his knowledge, a movement in the church which would have been you. Then you leaned over and a stone fell from a gargoyle. But you were terrified and backed away and hid. You did not see what happened.'

Mr Grindle-Ford had spun a wintry web around Jessie. But Sir Rudyard Warmley made a shimmering dazzling web of tight silk to catch his victim. He smiled gently at John.

'Yes, sir,' said John, who completely trusted him.

'A stone mason has examined the gargoyle and all is as you say,' said Sir Rudyard, in his warm cawing drowsy voice. 'But you should have owned up, my boy—'

John hung his head. He'd heard enough of that from the little voice. But Mr Justice Sparrow piped up from his perch high above the Court.

'Sir Rudyard! If you please! IF you please! You are here to look at evidence and not to pass judgement. That is my task, Sir Rudyard.'

'I apologize, m'lord,' said Sir Rudyard blinking. His gentle cawing turned to soft cooing like a sleepy wood pigeon. Lots of questions for John to answer. 'When had he first met the navvyman? Had he ever seen him drunk? Had he ever seen him violent? Had he ever given him money? Was he frightened of him?'

'I was a bit, sir.'

'Thank you, Mellor. You may stand down.' If he had been able to pat John like a stray wild dog, he would have. He'd nearly got what he wanted. There was a pause while some dusty snake-like whispering rustled in the heat.

Then they put Jessie in the witness box. She saw John for the first time. The smile she gave him was like the sun after cold spring rain. Sir Rudyard seemed to want to let her smile at John. It was part of his reptilian plan. He arranged papers, pretended to have lost one, while she smiled at John and he smiled back.

'Please question the witness, Sir Rudyard. The Court has

not got all day. Justice must be done.' Mr Justice Sparrow looked ruffled.

'Of course, m' lord.' He seemed to find the paper he wanted. Sir Rudyard talked as softly to Jessie as he would a frightened kitten. Yes. All she had wanted to do was to save John. She had just run with the fallen stone. She knew he would be in terrible trouble. Sir Rudyard coaxed everything out of her. She relaxed like a kitten in a pool of sun.

'You should have stayed to help the old man too,' said Sir Rudyard gently.

'You are passing judgements again, Sir Rudyard!' chirped the Judge. 'Kindly leave that to me.' The thin bird-black legs swung to and fro irritably under his robes. He wanted to get on with it and quickly sentence the guilty.

Then Sir Rudyard placed Miss Fanny Gibbs in the box. Fanny began to weep silently. But they were not bitter secretive sobs. A weight had been lifted from her by the handsome Mr Taylor. He had told her that everything would be all right. She smiled at him across the court and then at Sir Rudyard who began to question her.

Yes. She had seen somebody else in the churchyard when she saw Jessie running away. It was a figure on the tower. But she was uncertain who it was . . . she had thought it was John but she had not been certain . . . she did not want to get John into trouble when she was not sure who it was. Fanny was a splendid liar. Her body swaying, her tears trickling, her little catches of the breath. 'I didn't want to get poor John into any trouble . . . I was a little frightened you see . . . there had been so many strange tales of stone devils and ghosts from the children . . . the moon was in my eyes . . . '

'And what beautiful eyes!' thought Sir Rudyard. She had said exactly what he had wanted. He beamed at her. He twiddled his gown tape while he made sure that the Jury saw her beauty, just as he had let the Jury see Jessie's smile for John.

'Thank you, Miss Gibbs,' said Sir Rudyard. His smile to her was the one he used for the young ladies who were the Queen's guests at her Garden parties at Windsor, where he was a regular visitor. It was quite unlike the smile he had

173

used on Jessie and John, which was a smile he used for animals. He watched Miss Fanny Gibbs leave the box. She had a dress of moss-green silk and matching parasol. She was wearing crystal drop ear-rings and a straw hat trimmed with yellow and white poppies. 'Her tears are like raindrops on a summer field,' thought Sir Rudyard.

Then the avalanche that Fanny had set in motion that January day began to rumble again, seeking its victim. The Judge's eyes hardened and became cold points of frosty stars instead of summer ones. The sleepy jackdaws began to seek something to thrust their sharp beaks into. The snake rustling in the hot court began to boil and hiss. Sir Rudyard, who had been so nice to the children, began to get nastier and nastier to Handsome Jack, who had now become somebody with the ordinary name of John Buxton. Questions were spat at him, hisses of disbelief were aimed at him. Mr Justice Sparrow became as alert as a fighting cock and leaned forward with bird-like eye on Handsome Jack. Sir Rudyard suddenly lifted his arm, and with his gown and arm outstretched roared, 'Silence!' And there was. Then in a dangerous voice Sir Rudyard made a speech to Handsome Jack.

'It is my belief, prisoner at the bar, that you saw the old man, Ezekiel Dobson, counting his money when you called in the shop. Your visit there has been described by John Mellor and Jessie Smith. Then you followed the old man into the churchyard of All Saints, Lambton, where the unfortunate and innocent old gentleman had gone to place a tribute of snowdrops upon the grave of his dear departed wife. Once in the graveyard, you saw the stone fall from the tower and wound the old man. You witnessed the foolish and misguided bravery of Jessie Smith, when you saw her running away with the stone in a brave attempt to save her sweetheart from trouble. There you saw your chance.'

He stared at Handsome Jack, his arm outstretched, the silk sleeve of his gown shimmering in the heat of the court. Mr Justice Sparrow leaned forward like a small bird on a rooftop watching a dangerous cat far below, his bird eyes frost bright and very very interested in Handsome Jack.

There was a hot deep silence in the courtroom, like the pause before a thunderstorm.

'You saw your chance. You stepped forward and picked up a stone. You brought it down on the old man's head with great force and you killed the old man at once. Then you stole his gold with a cold-hearted abandon and you have been spending that gold freely ever since. Later, when you were questioned by the poor young guilty Mellor, you told him foolish stories about stone devils, knowing, in your evil cunning, that all children in the town had been telling each other stories about stone devils, ghosts and other phantasmagoria. You knew that the young boy would believe you and support your foolish idea. You thought to prove your innocence by telling John Mellor this stupid tale. All the time it was you, prisoner, that killed the old man. You may have fooled John Mellor. But you do not fool m' learned friends, m' lord and the rest of this worthy Court.'

So the avalanche of the law was on the move again, and Handsome Jack was in the way of it now Jessie had been moved aside. But Handsome Jack had no friends to shield, no love in his life. He roared at the engulfing avalanche like a threatened animal. The rook men cawed at him, charged him, nodded, and he roared back. Mr Justce Sparrow wrote pages of notes, his quill appearing to shake to the thunder of voices in the courtroom. John shivered and trembled. He saw the power and strength in Handsome Jack, and fully expected Handsome Jack to leap across the courtroom like an avenging giant and throttle him in rage. John had never expected this to happen. He was near to tears, for part of him greatly liked the giant. Jessie sat totally absorbed in John, her face flushed with pleasure at the sight of him. Her dreams had come true. Fanny divided her time between looking at the handsome Mr Taylor and, to her eyes, the equally desirable John. She did not spare a thought for the roaring, sweating, terrified giant Handsome Jack during the next two hours.

'I stole his gold! Right, I stole 'is gold, I stole his gold,' yelled Jack. 'But a devil came and killed him first, a devil dressed in black, a devil with a black cloak an' a white bone face—'

It was like a lion roaring at vultures as they circled him, wheeling ever closer to the moment when the giant would be killed. All this time Mr Justice Sparrow's quill was on the move, for he was a scribbler, unlike Mr Justice Gault who had been a finger wagger. As he wrote, his little thin legs trembled in their black silk stockings under his fine robes, and now and again he rubbed his legs together with excitement.

Handsome Jack bellowed and raged. He split the wood in the dock and John went white with fear. He felled two policemen, knocking one to the ground with a furious blow. Nails and screws from the wood were scattered like hail in a summer storm. But it was all of no use.

Out came the black cap. Handsome Jack was duly sentenced to death for the murder of Ezeliel Dobson.

Then Jessie was outside in fresh air, crying and laughing between Mr Taylor and Mr Rhodes, the westering sunlight turning her tears to gold on her pale prison face. She cried aloud when she heard the birds sing, for this was the first free air she had breathed for five months. They let her hug John. Mr Rhodes was to look after her. He had been given money by Emma Briddon to help the poor child. Mr Taylor wanted to help too. Jessie Smith was now a symbol of his success. So Jessie ran about on the steps of the court like a kitten let out to play. The golden warmth of the May afternoon poured down on her thin figure in the prison dress three sizes too big.

Mr Taylor called for a cab and they set off for the station, John, Jessie, Mr Taylor, and shabby Mr Rhodes in his frayed minister's gown. The cab window was open and the sun streamed in on their faces. Three of them were crying, Mr Rhodes, Jessie and John. Mr Taylor did not cry. He patted instead. But the tears were warm in the sunshine as it streamed through the little rattling window, their sobs became one with the happy trotting of the horse, and between the sobs they all breathed in the air of golden freedom scented with the dust of the streets, horses, straw and lilac from the gardens.

Inside the court there was a hot stifling hell. There were no warm tears being shed in there. Just the simple revenge of the law. And Handsome Jack would hang on Midsummer Day.

CHAPTER
[29]

A FEW days later, a cold dark figure of grief hurried down
the hot white road from One Ash to Lambton. Her face was
white and as she walked she stared at the white dust of the
road, as though hoping to warm her cold heart from the
reflected sun. Not once did she look around her at the froth of
hawthorn blossom above the white limestone walls, or see
the hot suns of the roadside dandelions. None of the gold
and white of the May day reached her. Her skin was a
deathly white, stretched over her face so that it looked like
ivory or white thin bone. It was Emma Briddon going
about her business.

She went straight to Mr Taylor's office and accepted the
glass of port he gave her. He gently pulled the white linen
blind down to stop the fierce May sun from shining on her
black clothes of mourning. How tragic that she had
mourned her dead sister for all these years. How she must
have loved her, thought Mr Taylor. He waited till she had
finished the wine, then he presented her with the bill for
helping Jessie Smith. It was a large one. But she did not
appear to want to talk of her kindness in helping the girl.
That was the mark of a true gentlewoman, thought Mr
Taylor as he watched her count the gold sovereigns from
her black silk purse embroidered with purple lilies of death.
A ray of sun flashed under the blind.

'Please draw the blind further, Mr Taylor. I do not wish
the light to shine on me.'

'Of course, Miss Briddon.' She went on counting the
gold.

Neither did she wish to know the details about the rogue
and scoundrel, John Buxton, who had been sentenced to

death for the murder of her brother-in-law. Indeed, she had become quite agitated when he told her, and licking her bloodless lips she had risen from her chair before his clerk had returned with the receipt for the gold. But no matter, it could be sent by post. No matter.

'I bid you good day, Miss Briddon,' said Mr Taylor as she hurried out. 'You have acted with great charity and Christian understanding to help Jessie Smith so.' Emma Briddon made a small sound as she left, but what it meant Mr Taylor never knew. He watched her hurry across the sunlit square, a strange wintry figure in the gold of the day.

From Mr Taylor's she made her way to the stone mason's yard in Water Lane.

'How is the stone slab, monument to my brother-in-law, coming along? I want it in position by Midsummer Day you know.' She rubbed her dry hands together nervously.

'Us've got the black marble you asked for, Miss Briddon, ma'am and work on the gold leaf lettering is nearly finished. The lettering is cut but the gold leaf hasn't been done yet.'

'Let me see.'

She traced the letters on the expensive black marble with one white finger.

'There's just one thing, Miss Briddon, ma'am.'

'Yes?'

'You just wanted the words VENGEANCE IS MINE on the bottom of the slab. What it should be, if you don't mind me telling you ma'am, is 'Vengeance is mine, saith the Lord'. I hope you don't mind me telling you, ma'am.' He cleared his throat nervously. 'It's a good text, ma'am, if you don't mind me telling you, seeing as the late Mr Dobson were murdered, like.' He stopped. The look on her face was murderous.

'I asked you to carve VENGEANCE IS MINE. That is what I want. If you cannot do my bidding I shall take my trade elsewhere. You will do it as I asked. Or not at all. I want VENGEANCE IS MINE and nothing else. Do you understand me, Mr Clay?'

'Yes, ma'am,' said the mason, backing away. The lady was still upset by the murder and everything, he thought.

'I want that stone in place on Midsummer Day, Mr Clay. I shall not be here. But I want to know the stone will be in place for everyone to see on that day.'

She swirled out of the yard, her head held high. The stone mason admired her. He thought it was a marvellous idea to have the marble slab put up on the day they would hang the man for Throttlepenny's murder. 'Vengeance is mine,' he muttered. 'Aye. 'Er's right. I'll see to it mysen that the stone goes up at the exact time they hang that navvyman in Derby.'

CHAPTER
[30]

IT WAS another golden day but even lovelier, in June, and it was Market Day in Lambton. John was waiting to speak to Fanny. He stood in the warm velvet shadows outside the main door to the school. He knew she would be coming out soon. The brick of the school sent out waves of warmth, and the scent of dust, pigs, horses, hay and roses wafted around John as he lounged against the warm brick, whistling softly, a straw between his teeth.

Fanny emerged at half-past four. She rustled out in cool pink silk with the usual straw hat decorated with red ribbons and red carnations. Her face had softened again now the terrible wintry burden had gone, and she looked more beautiful than ever.

As Fanny appeared John went up to her. It was the first time he had seen her alone since the trial. He placed his hands on her shoulders and kissed her lightly on her lips before she could do anything.

'Thanks, Fan, for trying to save me,' he said gruffly.

John was all spruced up again. He was wearing a clean shirt and new corduroys. His boots were clean. He was carrying a new cap in his hand as near to the type Handsome Jack had worn as he could find. His hair was sleek and shining from a Market Day visit to the Lambton barber. The barber had removed the fluff from his chin. His eye was as bright as ever. Mr Rhodes had wisely thought that a complete new job was needed, and had found John work on a large farm on the Staffordshire border with Derbyshire, just above the River Manifold, five miles to the west of Mr Rhodes' chapel and the railway where John and Handsome Jack had worked together. The farm had a large

181

team of shire horses and John was given the job of looking after these great horses that pulled the ploughs and harrows. Mr Rhodes had found Mrs Mellor a cottage in One Ash, close by Emma Briddon. John walked the seven miles every Sunday to see his mother. Now John was here in Lambton. He had brought a horse to the Lambton farrier, who was going to examine a slight loss of hair on the horse's coat. John's master was a kindly man, a great admirer of Mr Rhodes. He was giving John an easy time for the next few months, with trips to markets, farriers, black-smiths, and long days of sunshine in the fields haymaking.

Fanny's legs turned to water at the kiss. She had actually been in his arms for a few seconds and he did not hate her. She had felt his strong arms through her dress. She liked the smell of the new velveteen jacket he had bought and put on for the trip to market. Fanny went a deep red. She felt a surge of love. Then hate. All the trouble he'd caused her. He should have owned up. And why hadn't he smiled at her in court like he had at Jessie Smith? She hated him. No, she loved his strong arms. No, she hated him. What would people think? What if Middlemas saw? She smacked his face—hard.

But he looked at her with no hatred and his eyes met hers. She felt her throat swell. She could not breathe properly.

'It's still thanks, Fan. I'll never forget. What you tried to save me from . . . ' He'd backed away. There was a red mark on his cheek. Fanny wanted him to kiss her again. There was a giggle from behind the door. It was a girl from Standard Nine in the cloakroom.

'Come out, Eliza Thompson, you little spy,' snapped Fanny. She marched Eliza back inside the schoolroom, and fetched the Punishment Book with its gold leaf facsimile lettering and black shining covers. Fanny wrote in it.

| Eliza Thompson | For eavesdropping | A stern reprimand. |

When Fanny returned outside, John had gone.

John whistled as he rode the big shire horse he had

collected from the farrier's. He did not want to be late. He knew his master was being kind to him and he did not wish to take advantage of him. On his way back he would call on Jessie. Mr Rhodes had found a place on a farm for Jessie too. He did not think it was right for her to have to live in the town where she had once, however wrongly, been put in court. Jessie now lived on a farm on the upper part of the River Dove, in the next valley to John's. The farm was tucked cosily into a fold of the valley, and sheltered from the cruel east wind of winter by a little wood. Jessie had been given the job of dairy maid there. Mr Rhodes had thought the farm was a place to forget old miseries, with the sparkling river below and the green hills stretching into eternity. He was right. At the farm Jessie found kindness, farm dogs and puppies, cats and kittens, horses and foals, and butter making for Ashbourne Market, Leek Market and Lambton. Her days were happy ones of making butter, looking after young animals, and visits to markets down flower-filled lanes. She had a room of her own at the top of the house, filled with sun by day and her old friend the moon at night. On Sunday she went home to Lambton, with butter and cheese for her bewildered mother, and little toys she had sewn from scraps for her brothers. For the first time in her short life Jessie was beginning to sing as she worked.

Sometimes, like today, John called to see her. The farmer and his wife did not mind. They let her see him in the kitchen and always had things to do somewhere else when he did come. Today he had brought her a red ribbon from the market and a bunch of pinks to put with it in her sunbonnet.

But both John and Jessie felt sad as Midsummer Day approached. The farms used to lend each other farm hands to help with getting in the hay. Now it was the day before Midsummer Day and John was at Jessie's farm helping to fetch in the last load of hay. That afternoon and evening there would be a party to celebrate the fine hay harvest of a good and heavy early crop.

Mr Rhodes had called at the farm, where he was always welcome, and he had given thanks to God to see John and Jessie so happy.

Now it was six o'clock on Midsummer Eve, and golden sunshine was still pouring down on John and Jessie, warming them with its radiance as though the winter of sorrow had never been. Jessie had put on a new print sundress and in her bonnet she was wearing the red silk ribbon and some pinks, because John liked the ribbon. She was not so keen on it. The red reminded her of the Judge's robes. But thoughts like that were coming less and less.

People were kind and left them to themselves. They were sitting apart from the others under a big ash tree, and they'd eaten pork pie, hard-boiled eggs and salad, and now they were eating Mrs James's plum cake and washing it down with ginger beer. Mrs James was the farmer's wife who smiled on Jessie. Neither she nor Mr James allowed beer or other alcohol on the farm.

John smiled at Jessie. Her face was now a soft brown in the sunshine, the colour of a light brown hen's egg, freshly laid. Her hair had lighter streaks in it, the same colour as Fanny Gibbs's. Jessie was smiling and full of cake. She had picked a red clover from under the hedge where it had escaped the scythes of the haymakers. She was pulling the red petals away from the stalk and sucking the sweet honey at the end of each petal. As she did so she chanted.

'You love me . . . you don't love me . . . you love me . . . you don't love me . . . ' John stared at her. She looked so fragile. How could he even have thought of letting her hang? He shifted himself closer to her in the sun that warmed him through and through. But he must not think like that. Mr Rhodes had told him to forget. He never would be able to. He moved as close to her as he dared. She'd got a hay stalk stuck in her hair and he tried to get it out with his teeth. They fell about laughing under the great friendly tree. Then John went quiet again. Jessie, sensing his every mood, sat up.

'John . . . what is it?'

'Nowt . . . it's just that it's Midsummer Day tomorrow and they'll hang Handsome Jack, and I still don't think he did it . . . he'd have gone right down south, gone right away if he had . . . he wouldn't have told me . . .'

Jessie felt sad though she could not fully understand John's sadness. He had rescued her, hadn't he? She felt sorry for the navvy but she had none of John's direct concern.

Then she gave a cry of joy. A stout figure, dressed in rusty black, was wheezing her way towards them. It was Mrs Sugg. Jessie leaped to her feet crying with pleasure and ran over to her. She wrapped her arms around the dusty hot black coat and rubbed her face against the comfort. Mrs Sugg, crying a little, hugged her tightly back.

'It's taken me three hours to get here, m' duck, from Derby. It's a right God-forsaken spot. I thought the train'd never make it right up into these hills. Or me for that matter. I'm not as young as I was. And I've only half an hour before I've got to go back for the train.'

Jessie led her over to where John and herself had been sitting. John found himself looking at the ground, ashamed of himself. This woman had looked after Jessie while he was being a coward.

'This is John,' said Jessie shyly. 'He left his job to come and rescue me and find out who really did it.' She buried herself in the comforting black again.

'Oh it is, is it? So this is John, is it?' Mrs Sugg remembered the Lambton gossip she had heard when she was looking for him. 'I'm glad I've met him at last, m' duck.' She stared at John for a full minute. Then she hugged Jessie even tighter as though to protect her from what she saw. Then she carried on staring at John.

John shuffled. He blushed to the roots of his sun-bleached coppery red hair. He felt he was being stared at with all-seeing eyes. Eyes that saw his cowardice. Eyes that saw the number of times he had run away from saving Jessie. Eyes that saw, and knew that if he had not found Handsome Jack when he had, he would have let Jessie hang rather than own up. He nudged a wisp of hay with his boot. Mrs Sugg just stared.

Boys! Men! she thought. They get away with murder . . . Then she realized what she had thought and how near to the truth it might have been, and she shivered. She held Jessie tighter than ever. She sensed that John had only just saved the situation and that he was very ashamed of himself. She could see the tears shining in his downcast eyes.

John was terrified she was going to say something about his cowardice.

Mrs Sugg never took her eyes off him. And what made her blood boil was that she knew Jessie would not have the worthless scallywag any other way. She sniffed. Perhaps when Jessie was her age, women would not let men get away with so much. And why should they? Women and girls were no different from men. Better in some ways she thought. Well, she could see the lad was ashamed of his part in it all, whatever it was. They said he'd been looking for the navvy all that time. Well, she knew a liar when she saw one.

Mrs Sugg never took her eyes off John. She munched plum cake, held Jessie, shook hands with the farmer and his wife, and stared and stared at John. Then she held Jessie to her, her boots sticking out in the hay stubble. But she still looked at John. She felt drowsy in the slanting sun. She half closed her eyes. She could hear Jessie's heart beating. She sighed. Perhaps in a hundred years from now, in 1985, she thought, girls would not believe everything boys said.

She opened her eyes wide to wither the worthless John with one more scorching stare. Worthless streak o' lightning in breeches, she thought.

She got up at last to go. She spoke to John for the first time.

'And this time take care of her. Or you'll have me to contend with.' Jessie, still hugging her, did not understand. But John did, every word. He nodded but could not look her straight in the eyes.

They said goodbye and there was a faint sadness in the golden air. Mrs Sugg toiled up the long white lane to the little station thinking about the wickedness of men. Jessie was sad because she sensed John was. John was miserable because of Mrs Sugg's looks and the fact that Handsome Jack would die tomorrow.

The last evening of Handsome Jack's life drew to its close. The sun sank in a golden haze over the hills and seemed to rest there, as though reluctant to leave the scene it saw. John walked home content but with the deep sadness of the execution in him still. The last of the sun shone on him, turning the clouds of gnats around him into a golden halo, turning the wild roses into golden roses as they bloomed on the old stone walls. The warm last rays of the sun dried the tears on his cheeks as he walked back to the farm. There was at least one person in the world who would miss Handsome Jack.

Mr Rhodes walked home too. He saw John's figure dwindle into the radiance of the sunset and he too was overcome with a strange sadness. He knew Handsome Jack was guilty, but he did not believe in hanging. When John was out of sight up the long winding road, Mr Rhodes knelt down in the clover and bedstraw under a wall and prayed for John Buxton. Then he got up and decided that the best way to feel comfort was to give comfort. He would go and see Emma Briddon. She had been worrying him a great deal lately. She looked ill. She appeared to have taken the dreadful business of her brother-in-law's murder very much to heart. He would go and see her now, late as it was. On the eve of the guilty man's execution, she might like to say a prayer with him. It would comfort them both.

The sun had set and the church clock at One Ash was striking nine when he knocked at her cottage door. While he waited, he admired the fine pink roses that grew round the porch. Each had a heart of gold the colour of the western sky.

'Are you there, Miss Briddon?'

But there was no answer. He trudged back to his lonely chapel and tiny cottage. He was exhausted. He tried to pray and could not. There was a small voice inside him, tormenting him. Mr Rhodes believed this small voice was the voice of God and always listened to it. Tonight the little voice was telling him to return and see Emma Briddon.

Sighing with exhaustion, Mr Rhodes obeyed. He put on

his suit and his gown. He had no time to brush it. The little voice nagged and nagged. He must go now. Now. At once.

He hurried up the long white road, glimmering with the light from the midnight sun buried deep under the hills to the north. A few faint stars added to the moth-like light of the midsummer night.

When he got to the cottage he went in. He stood still in the parlour, listening. What did God want him to do next? The little voice said nothing. So he stood and waited. Emma's grandfather clock ticked on and struck three. An owl called. A board creaked. The church clock struck three. Then he noticed a glimmer of white in the gloom. It was a letter on the red cloth of the table. He held it close to his tired eyes. But he could not read the name on it.

He fumbled in his pockets for matches and struck one. The letter was addressed to him. The match went out so he struck another and lit a candle in a silver candlestick. He ripped open the letter. He read it, then he stuffed it in his pocket and leaving the candle burning he ran out of the cottage, his heart beating wildly. He must reach Derby before they hanged Handsome Jack.

CHAPTER
[31]

EMMA BRIDDON had been a tormented woman for the last few weeks. She hardly dared go to sleep for fear of seeing Ezekiel's battered face staring up at her. As Midsummer Day approached, the haunting seemed to get worse. On the high hill in these long June nights it hardly seemed to get dark. The long nights shimmered with a white light. If she went to bed and drew her curtains, his battered face would appear in the tiny little cast-iron grate in her bedroom fireplace, his wounds glowing like blood behind the fire bars. If she got out of bed to wash her hands in the water bowl, she would see his battered face staring up at her there from the candlelit circle of water. It was always accusing her. And as Midsummer Day approached and she knew she would be to blame for another death, the face of her brother-in-law grew more accusing still. Not once did she think of going to Derby and telling the truth. Like John, her fear of the hangman's rope was too great.

It was worse when she went outside on these long June days. She would see the old man's face in the hawthorn blossom which was still blowing on these high hills. A white face with the trickle of scarlet blood.

She became a regular sight for the haymakers that year. They saw her as they set off for the fields at four o'clock in the morning, their scythes over their shoulders. They would hear the tunk-tunk of her pump as they watched her washing her hands there. They saw her staring at trees and bushes when they rested from the high June sun, as she walked the lonely hill roads. But they thought her a lady, and ladies were always allowed to behave a little differently.

As Midsummer Day approached she could stand it no

189

longer. She would never have believed it possible that one thought could fill her mind, night and day, but it did. Wherever she went, whatever she did, the thought never left her. There was always the little voice. 'You have killed Ezekiel.' There was no blame. There was no advice. Just those four words always there. It was the worst punishment on earth. She needed no other. Her life was smashed by these four words. She could stand it no more.

Eight o'clock on Midsummer Eve saw her writing a letter to Mr Rhodes, her quill pen scratching in the last of the golden light coming through her parlour window.

She would leave the letter on the parlour table. The minister would find it one day. When she had written it, she would leave for ever.

> *Rose Cottage*
> *One Ash*
> *Derbyshire*
> *Midsummer Eve   1885*
>
> *Dear Mr Rhodes,*
> *I have sinned and I can no longer live with my sin.*
>
> *I killed my brother in law Ezekiel Dobson. God forgive me. Since he killed my dear sister Letitia with his cruel ways and meanness I have hated him.*
> *I think I was possessed by a devil that night in January. I saw Ezekiel slip as he approached the grave of my darling sister, and God forgive me I laughed out loud. Then soon after I saw a stone fall on him and I laughed again. I do not know why.*
>
> *I saw the girl run with the stone as though she had done it, and I laughed to see him clutch his head.*
>
> *Earlier I had seen a tramp go into the porch as I waited in the shadows. I did not want to be seen by Ezekiel. Seeing the old fool dazed by the stone, I fetched the tramp. I suddenly wanted to hurt the man who had caused me so much pain. A devil came into my mind and told me how. I kept laughing. My mind was taken over by a devil. I picked up a stone and hit Ezekiel over his head. I hit him hard. It had the force of fifty years' hatred Then I emptied Ezekiel's pockets of much gold and gave it to the poor . . .*

Mr Rhodes read no more. He stuffed the letter in his pocket and ran from the cottage. For a time he ran down the road to Summer Hay and its little station. He thought of running down the tracks to Ashbourne and getting a ride to Derby. Then, in his panic, he thought of running to Lambton and waving down a train. But he had no money and it would take an hour to get there, and he did not know if there was a train. He changed direction yet again and plunged into a field where the old hill lane led south to the town. He ran through the fields, his gown collecting heavy dew from dew-laden moonpenny daisies and sorrel. This would take him half-way or more, thence he might get a ride, hire a horse, see a train . . . rouse a J.P. He threw off his black gown and left it hanging on a thorn tree black against the white blossom like a giant ghost of a rook. He fell . . . he kneeled in prayer . . . his heart was beating wildly. He drank deeply from a field trough of water, watched by a friendly mild-eyed cow . . . he threw off his jacket and left it in a barn . . . now there was a light in the east the colour of Emma Briddon's roses, with a heart of gold where the sun would soon appear. He must get there, he must . . . The larks were rising . . . he mopped his brow, where sweat was pouring off. Field after field . . . it was downhill now all the way to Derby . . . he took his boots off and ran wildly over the prickly stubble of a mown hay field. The light in the east grew and swelled like a huge expanding rose of pink. Above him a thin moon appeared like a segment of lemon rind caught in the giant rose petals in the sky. He must save Handsome Jack . . . the man had had no life, no chance to let God speak to him. He dropped the letter, picked it up and prayed . . . God in his mercy would help. He began to cough and a pain in his chest tore at him . . . spare me, oh God, spare me . . . He was on a long road and there was a cart coming down it. He sank to his knees and waited for the cart.

CHAPTER
[32]

THE GREAT pink rose of the sunrise is blossoming over Derby Gaol. The rose has a heart of pure gold that is the sun in all its midsummer beauty rising to celebrate the middle of summer. As the sun rises the whole gaol is rinsed and renewed in golden warmth.

In a pool of early light the prison chaplain adjusts his black silk gown. It is sleekly black, unlike the dusty tatters of Mr Rhodes' gown. This gown is a hard Punishment Book black.

People are already moving around the prison. All appear to be very busy. Some seem to be very important people indeed. All are unsmiling even though the sky is like a giant pink flower and the sun is warm and good to feel. They all seem very determined. There is a sort of grim pleasure in the midsummer air. After all, justice is being done, isn't it?

There are crowds in the little street outside. Some have been there all the soft white midsummer night through. They seem very excited. A woman in a dirty shawl is selling coffee from a big jug for a penny a cup, with spirits two pence. She is doing a lot of talking. She is very excited. She can remember when there were hangings in public and she would like that to happen again. Things are not what they were.

In the prison they are taking the prisoner to the Pinioning Room. It is a low hot stuffy hellish hut, near to the scaffold where the prisoner will hang. The prisoner's hands are tied. Outside in the morning is the Hangman. He waits, all calm and still. He does not look up to the sky that is now a golden rose, and he takes no notice of a blackbird singing its pleading song on the high wall.

A procession begins. It starts with the High Sheriff of Derbyshire and the prison warden. Then comes the prisoner. The prisoner holds a bunch of flowers tightly. A boy sent them to him yesterday. They are from a midsummer field. There are big red clovers, moonpenny daisies, buttercups, sorrel, purple vetch, a foam of seeding grasses, and some orchids that were then very common. This is the only colour in the procession. Behind walks the chaplain, the Hangman, a doctor . . .

The prisoner climbs the steps to a high platform that is the scaffold. The procession follows. They do not look up. The flower in the sky has vanished. The sky is now like a huge inverted bluebell, so deep, so rich, so glorious. The flowers and the sky are beautiful.

The Hangman checks that the prisoner's hands are securely tied. A hood is placed over the prisoner.

The chaplain steps forward and reads the Burial Service. He has a pleasing voice and likes to use it. The prisoner is still. All goes well until the words in the Burial Service: 'Man that is born of woman hath a short time to live and is full of misery . . . He cometh up and is cut down like a flower . . .'

The flowers fall from the prisoner's hand. There is a struggle and some shouting and the blackbird flies from the wall. The sky seems to be getting bluer.

The prisoner is calmed. The Burial Service ends. The noose is put round the prisoner's neck. The prisoner is now crying. The clocks of Derby strike seven. The Hangman pulls a lever. There is a violent crash. A trapdoor opens under the prisoner's feet and the prisoner swings dead on the end of the rope.

A black flag is brought out of a dusty cupboard. It is hoisted up and flies over the gaol. It is an ugly stain on the midsummer blue. It is covered in dust and in the strong morning sunshine the flag seems shot with gold, like the gold and black of the Punishment Book that fascinates the children in far-off Lambton.

The doctor examines the prisoner and certifies him dead. The body of the prisoner is placed in a cheap wooden coffin. The bunch of flowers is thrown in with the body. Then the coffin is tipped into a pit of quick-lime in the corner of the prison grounds, where they bury people who have been hanged there.

Outside in the road, half an hour later, a shabby little figure is seen running down the road. He stops still when he sees the stain of the flag upon the pure summer sky. He falls to his knees in the road. He takes out a letter and slowly tears it into tiny shreds and puts the bits down a road drain.

Then he prays for love, forgiveness and the vanquishing of the Devil and all his works in the world.

EPILOGUE

ALL SAINTS Church in Lambton had been seriously shaken by earth tremors in the autumn of 1884. After the Archdeacon of Lambton, Dr Ball, heard about the falling stone, he had masons to check carefully all the old carvings and gargoyles that were on the church.

On inspection many of the gargoyles were found to be very dangerous and they were removed. They were carted away to an old disused quarry near One Ash. They were tipped to the bottom of it. Dr Ball thought the carvings both rude and ugly and did not want them kept in or near the church. On the other hand, he thought it would be most improper to have the stones broken up and used to repair roads. Dumping them in a lonely quarry seemed the best idea.

The quarry had a deep pool in it and Dr Ball was pleased to hear from the carter that the old carvings had been tipped into this deep pool. There had been a violent storm at the end of April that had quite spoiled the children's maypole dance, but this had filled the old workings up with deep water. It seemed a suitable place to get rid of the old half heathen things.

Soon after sunrise on Midsummer Morning, after a night of guilty and tormented wandering, Emma Briddon came to the quarry. She stood on the high cliff above the deep pool, a tragic and tormented figure. She looked down into the pool and seemed to see in its depths a devilish face, perhaps the devil that had made her laugh and do the terrible things she had done. A few seconds later, as though she were again possessed by a devil, she destroyed herself by throwing herself into the deep pool where the stone devil was waiting.

For a few moments the circle of blue was shattered with ugly dark ripples like black stains on the blue. Then Emma was seen no more.

The pool settled. The larks sang on. In the fields to the west of the quarry and in the Manifold Valley, the farmers began to cut their hay and another Harvest Home Party was arranged for the workers.

Mr Rhodes never did tell the truth. Rightly or wrongly, he thought everybody had suffered enough. The little voice that always guided him told him he had done the right thing.

In 1887 the law at last allowed young adults and children to be put on probation, instead of putting them in prisons and giving them adult punishments. But the law on hanging children was not abolished until 1908, when children could no longer be hanged in Great Britain. Hanging adults in Great Britain was finally abolished in 1965. There are a lot of people who would like to see the death penalty return for grown-up people.

Chandra

Frances Mary Hendry
ISBN 0 19 275058 5
Winner of the Writer's Guild Award and the Lancashire
Book Award

Chandra can't believe her luck. The boy her parents have chosen for her to marry seems to be modern and open-minded. She's sure they will have a wonderful life together. So once they are married she travels out to the desert to live with him and his family—only when she gets there, things are not as she imagined.

Alone in her darkened room she tries to keep her strength and her identity. She is Chandra and she won't let it be forgotten.

River Boy

Tim Bowler
ISBN 0 19 275035 6
Winner of the Carnegie Medal

Standing at the top of the fall, framed against the sky, was the figure of a boy. At least, it looked like a boy, though he was quite tall and it was hard to make out his features against the glare of the sun. She watched and waited, uncertain what to do, and whether she had been seen.

When Jess's grandfather has a serious heart attack, surely their planned trip to his boyhood home will have to be cancelled? But Grandpa insists on going so that he can finish his final painting, 'River Boy'. As Jess helps her ailing grandfather with his work, she becomes entranced by the scene he is painting. And then she becomes aware of a strange presence in the river, the figure of a boy, asking her for help and issuing a challenge that will stretch her swimming talents to the limits. But can she take up the challenge before it is too late for Grandpa . . . and the River Boy?

Flambards

K. M. Peyton
ISBN 0 19 275024 0

Twelve-year-old Christina is sent to live in a decaying old mansion with her fierce uncle and his two sons. She soon discovers a passion for horses and riding, but she has to become part of a strange family. This brooding household is divided by emotional undercurrents and cruelty . . .

Chartbreak
Gillian Cross
ISBN 0 19 275043 7

When Janis Finch storms out of a family row, it starts a chain of events which transforms her whole life. For it's in the motorway café, minutes later, that she meets the unknown rock band, Kelp, who talk her into coming to their gig that night.

Janis goes along for the ride, and finds herself increasingly provoked by Christie, Kelp's arrogant lead singer. He pushes her into singing with them, and winds her up into a fever of rage, awe, and attraction. So when Christie asks her to join the band, Janis feels powerless to refuse—and her life explodes.

A Pack of Lies
Geraldine McCaughrean
ISBN 0 19 275016 X
Winner of the Carnegie Medal and the Guardian Children's Fiction Award

Ailsa Povey doesn't trust MCC Berkshire, the mysterious man helping out in her mother's antique shop. He dazzles every customer with enchanting stories about the antiques, but Ailsa knows it's all a big pack of lies.

Yet still the stories come thick and fast: tales of adventure, revenge, mystery, and horror. Now only one story remains to be told—that of MCC himself. Who is he? Where is he from? And, most importantly, what does he want from the Poveys?

A Haunted Year
Ann Phillips
ISBN 0 19 275046 1

Florence is bored. The Easter holidays are dragging on—until she finds a way to summon up a ghost.

Now she has a friend to play with. George always comes when she calls him. And soon she doesn't even need to call him. And then—he won't go away . . .

No matter what Florence does or where she goes, George is always there!